A Deadly
SOLUTION

A Tea & Sympathy Mystery

BOOK 2

J. NEW

A Deadly Solution
A Tea & Sympathy Mystery
Book 2

Cover design: J. New.
Interior formatting: Alt 19 Creative

OTHER BOOKS BY J. NEW

The Yellow Cottage Vintage Mysteries in order:
The Yellow Cottage Mystery (Free)
An Accidental Murder
The Curse of Arundel Hall
A Clerical Error
The Riviera Affair
A Double Life

The Finch & Fischer Mysteries in order:
Decked in the Hall
Death at the Duck Pond

Tea & Sympathy Mysteries in order:
Tea & Sympathy
A Deadly Solution
Tiffin & Tragedy

Chapter One

*L*ILLY TWEED, FORMER agony aunt now purveyor of fine teas at The Tea Emporium in Plumpton Mallet's market square, was currently sitting in Psychiatrist Dr Jorgenson's office. She had met him a few months prior when she'd made a phony appointment in order to question him about one of his patients. A woman who had died in what Lilly thought were suspicious circumstances. He'd been very gracious regarding her subterfuge and had answered those questions he could, within the remit of his profession, but toward the end he'd cleverly brought the conversation round to Lilly herself. Through their conversation she discovered she had been harbouring negative feelings and some fair amount of guilt regarding her divorce several years prior.

He'd recognised immediately she had been swallowing her emotions and putting on a brave face which as the years had gone by had become second nature. It had come as a complete surprise to Lilly, however. She and her ex-husband had eventually fallen into a platonic relationship, more house mates than partners, and had become lazy in their romantic endeavours, taking each other for granted, and they had naturally drifted apart. While one party wasn't to blame over the other, Lilly had shouldered more than her fair share of responsibility for the failed relationship. Alongside the proverbial, 'is it me?'

Falling out of love, they had gone their separate ways before the apathy could become animosity, and in the main it had been with little tension. He had moved away from Plumpton Mallet, making it easier for them both to move on with their lives. Yet, there was still something about the experience that had been quietly gnawing away at her, and it had taken Dr Jorgenson to make her see it.

He'd also made a diagnosis which could transform into something of a more serious nature if not addressed; compassionate empathy disorder. Lilly had never heard of it, but once Dr Jorgenson had explained what it was, she'd recognised it in herself immediately. It had come to the fore when she'd become reluctantly involved in solving the death of the local woman who had been the doctor's long-term patient.

"So what exactly is compassionate empathy disorder?" she'd asked when he'd first brought it up.

"Well, empathy itself is a significant human capability. It allows us to connect with one another, as well as recognise, understand and share in emotions."

"So, being able to react with compassion to what someone else is going through?"

"Exactly. But in some cases the person is very sensitive and highly tuned to others' emotions. This can result in 'empathy burnout,' which is when you become emotionally exhausted and completely overwhelmed by taking on everyone else's problems."

"And this is what I have?" Lilly had asked.

"Not quite yet, it's borderline, though. It would seem you do have difficulty regulating your emotions. If there isn't that boundary, then you risk taking it all on and going the other way. That's to say you tend to stop feeling so empathetic. Your empathy becomes your kryptonite, if you like, and can start to cause you harm. It's a challenge to step back from, but that's something I can help you work through."

It was at this point that Lilly had welcomed the opportunity to address her issues with the doctor, and regular therapy sessions were set up. He went on to explain in more detail the disorder.

"There are three categories of empathy; **Cognitive;** where you can place yourself in another's shoes, understand and relate to their emotions and react in an appropriate way. **Affective**; where you share the feelings another is experiencing. Becoming one with their emotions if you like. And finally, **Compassionate;** this incorporates both of the other types, making you want to take action and relieve the other person of their suffering. It's partly what made you such an effective agony aunt."

Over several sessions, they went on to discuss at length the emotional cost of Lilly's involvement in the death of Carol Ann Hotch. She had found herself several times mired in the guilt and emotional well-being of all those concerned.

From the victim herself, her husband, and the perpetrator. Even Abigail Douglas, the woman who had taken over her agony aunt job at the paper and was known to be an extremely difficult personality, didn't escape her innate feeling of compassion.

But it was Stacey, an American student and her employee, who had eventually come to her and Abigail's rescue at the eleventh hour, that she felt most responsible for. And it was to her that the conversation turned today, during her fourth session with Dr Jorgenson.

❦

"SO, TELL ME how things are going with Stacey? She's been with you a few months now." Lilly shifted in her chair and reached for a glass of water on the side table, taking a sip before answering.

"Well, now that the summer holidays are here, she's taken more hours at the shop as she's not got classes. She really is an excellent employee and the customers love her. I had been worried initially about her lack of knowledge regarding what I sell, but she's learned so much since she came to work for me. She said when she first applied that she was a quick study and she was right. My fears were totally unfounded. I couldn't be more pleased."

Dr Jorgenson smiled. "I expect her being on summer break has afforded you more free time than you're used to since you first opened?"

"Absolutely. I try not to take advantage of her and still spend most of my time in the shop. It is my business, after all. But I am a bit worried about Stacey."

"Worried? In what way?"

"It's her father," Lilly said. Wondering if she was about to be ticked off for getting involved in matters that weren't her concern. "She has dual citizenship and grew up in America with her mother because her father was unreliable. She chose to come to a university in England in order to get to know him better, yet he kept her at arms-length for the longest time. He didn't seem to want anything to do with her. He lives in London, I think I've mentioned that before?"

"It's a long way from here. Has he been to visit at all?"

"Not at first, but ever since the newspaper headline ran about how we solved Carol Ann's case, he turns up quite regularly."

Both Stacey and Lilly had ended up on the front page of The Plumpton Mallet Gazette when it was discovered they were instrumental in solving the case. Stacey had two black eyes, the result of a traffic accident which had ultimately ended a high-speed car chase, the likes of which the small town had never seen before, and saved Lilly's bacon. Along with that of Abigail Douglas who was driving the car being pursued. The sight of his daughter's injuries on-line had spurred Mr Pepper into action, and he'd immediately caught the first available train and landed in Lilly's shop the same afternoon.

"What is it that concerns you, exactly?" Dr Jorgensen asked after a lengthy pause. He never seemed to ask a question that he didn't at least suspect she already knew the answer to.

"I suppose I'm worried it's not sincere," Lilly said. "Stacey and I have become quite close since she started working for me, as well as also renting the flat above the shop, and I naturally care about her welfare. Mr Pepper has a tendency to let her down quite regularly whenever they make plans, and I'm worried it's causing her some stress."

The doctor made some notes then asked, "Have you tried to get to know Mr Pepper at all?" without looking up.

Lilly sighed. "No, not really. To be honest, I haven't actually wanted to. I find him quite taciturn and a bit belligerent."

Dr Jorgenson nodded as though that was exactly what he expected her to say. "Do you think perhaps, Lilly, the reason you are so concerned about the relationship between Mr Pepper and his daughter is because you are using Stacey as a stand in for your own lack of family in the area? Specifically, the fact that you and your ex-husband never had children of your own?"

Lilly started in shock. Her stomach dropped and her heart thumped. Then she frowned. She sometimes wondered why she came to see a man who kept holding up a mirror to her like this. Her parents had passed away, and she'd been an only child. While she'd grown up in Plumpton Mallet and had many friends, it was true she lacked a strong family connection. Drat it!

"I don't *believe* that's what I'm doing..." she said, then shook her head. "I don't know, maybe I am." It was a disconcerting admission.

"Don't get me wrong, Lilly, I think the relationship you've developed with Stacey is to be admired. There's nothing wrong with being a role model for the girl, and from what you've told me that's the kind of relationship you've developed. My concern is that Stacey already has both a mother and a father. Her own family drama to juggle. But it's her responsibility, not yours. It's wise not to overstep the mark and intertwine yourself in another's family matters."

Lilly folded her arms and looked down, tracing the pattern in the carpet with the toe of her sandal.

"Yes, you're right," she said eventually. "I don't want to overstep, Stacey and I have a good relationship, but I must remember that what's going on between her and her father is their business. I think being the agony aunt for Plumpton Mallet for so long has sometimes made me think people value and want my opinion or help more than they actually do. It's an issue of pride, isn't it? Another reason why I was sceptical initially about the idea of counselling. It was partly the irony of an agony aunt needing the services of a shrink."

Dr Jorgenson laughed. "It's good you recognise that about yourself." He closed his notebook and put his pen in his shirt pocket. The signal that the session was coming to an end.

They both stood up and Lilly grabbed her handbag from the adjacent chair, putting the strap over her shoulder.

"So, tell me, what's life been like since you became the most famous woman in Plumpton Mallet?"

Lilly chuckled. "Very strange. A couple of days ago I was away from the shop and Stacey told me later that four different people had come in looking for 'The Super Sleuth.' I've gone from being a local tea shop owner to a point of gossip or interest for over half the town. And beyond, actually. It's weird having people turn up at the shop wanting autographs or their photo taken with me, like I'm a character in a mystery book. It was over three months ago, yet people are still eating it up like it was yesterday. Even the tourists are aware of it. So much so that The Tea Emporium has now been added to the must see stops on the town tour."

"That must have been good for business?"

"It really has, and believe me I am not complaining, it's just not something I'm used to. Stacey loves it all though, and is now in charge of all our social media, which again has had a very positive effect on trade."

They'd walked as they talked and now found themselves at the door. Dr Jorgenson opened it for her and Lilly stepped out into the sunshine.

"I'll come and visit your shop soon," he said. "I'm an avid tea drinker."

"You wouldn't be British if you weren't," Lilly replied with a grin.

"Indeed. I need to find enough time to dedicate an hour or two in my pursuit of a perfect cup of tea."

"Well, you'll be made very welcome. You can try any sample I have. I'm sure we'll find your next favourite blend."

Lilly thanked the doctor and made her way down the small path. At the gate she turned left and within a couple of minutes was back out into the town centre, a few minutes' walk from the market square and her shop.

❦

THE SUMMER WAS now in full swing and the town centre was a hive of activity. Tour buses arrived daily, disgorging excited passengers eager to discover what this quaint little market town had to offer, and Plumpton Mallet had everything they could want.

The river, running along the outskirts of town, was flanked by large fields and small stony beaches, perfect for picnics, with designated areas for both swimming and fishing. The woods, a mass of bluebells carpeting the floor in the spring, were a joy to walk through in summer. Full of squirrels and songbirds and if you were very lucky, the odd deer. And the large green park with its avenue of trees, a play area for children and a pub with a cafe and outdoor seating at one end was immensely popular. As were the colourful rowing boats moored at the side of a quaint stone jetty, in the shadow of an ancient humped-backed foot bridge which took you over the river to the fields at the opposite side.

At the other side of the town were the moors, popular with walkers and hikers. Turning into a mass of purples and green in spring with the heather in abundance, it looked like an old master oil painting viewed from the town's market square nestled in the valley below. It was one of the most popular images for both photographs and on the postcards the town sold to tourists.

The cobbled market square was where Lilly's shop, The Tea Emporium, was situated. A prime position in the centre of the long row of historical shops that flanked one side, double fronted with a cream door in the centre. It looked both inviting and exciting. It also had the one thing none of the other shops had; a sleeping cat in the window. Earl Grey had been a stray who had wandered into the shop a week after it had opened and never left. Lilly adored him, especially because the scar across his nose and the missing chunk of his ear spoke volumes. Proof he'd had it tough on the streets but had survived.

Her bicycle, parked outside the shop and festooned with hanging baskets, looked an absolute picture, and several people had stopped to pose next to it to have their photos taken.

Inside, she checked the basket where her agony aunt letters, posted through the letterbox outside, were collected, and finding several tucked them under her arm. As her eyes adjusted to the dimmer light, compared to the blinding sunshine outside, she spotted Archie Brown, crime writer and her old colleague at the paper, having tea at the counter with Stacey.

Chapter Two

*I*T WAS RARE Lilly got a visit from Archie these days. With his additional workload due to the paper being taken over by a larger concern, a primary reason for Lilly being made redundant, he didn't have a lot of free time. But she was always happy to see him on those rare occasions when he did have enough for a cup of tea and a chat.

"Ah, the wanderer returns." Archie said with a smile. "We were about to give you up for lost."

"Hey, Lilly," Stacey said from the other side of the counter where she was brewing samples for some waiting customers.

Lilly smiled and spoke to several shoppers on her way through the shop, pleased to see it so busy.

"Hello you two. Nice to see you, Archie. What brings you in? Crime at an all-time low?"

Archie scoffed, "I wish. Actually, I was looking for some repair work," he said, pointing to a little teacup on a velvet covered board at the end of the counter. It was the area Lilly used for examining damaged items for repair. Fine china, delicate as it was, had a nasty habit of being mishandled and damaged, so this was an additional service she offered her customers. She'd taken numerous night classes and become very adept at it, but she only touched those items that weren't antiques or highly valuable.

"Let's have a look," she said, going behind the counter and searching through a drawer for her combined light and magnifying glass. After a close examination, she deemed it an easy repair. "There are no bits missing so a good adhesive, a light sand and a touch up and it will be as good as new."

"Excellent," Archie said. "I'm very fond of that tea set."

"I'm glad to hear it since you bought it from here."

"Best set I've ever owned, but I admit I should treat it with a bit more care. Now what's this little repair going to cost me?"

"Consider it a gift for a friend, Archie. It won't take me too long."

"Very kind of you, Lilly, thank you. Although I suppose you do owe me a favour."

Lilly raised an eyebrow. "Oh? And why is that, Archie Brown?"

"Two words," he said, holding up his fingers before folding his arms. "Abigail Douglas."

Lilly groaned. "What's she done now? And why is it my fault?"

"You persuaded me to let her co-write that last article. The greatest headline and story we've ever had. Since then, she's been the biggest headache you can imagine. She has ideas so far above her station I'm surprised she's not short of oxygen. Which actually would be a big improvement, come to think of it. She's driving everyone at the paper crazy with her demands for all the biggest projects, but especially me."

Lilly cringed. Abigail had started investigating the Carol Ann Hotch case behind Archie's back. She'd even swiped all his carefully researched notes. Because so few people wrote to the paper for Abigail's agony aunt column now, she had acted out of desperation and fear that her job was in jeopardy. However, Abigail had also been a great help to Lilly as she sought the truth and as a result Lilly had insisted Archie co-write the article with her, to give her some help and job security.

"I'm sorry," Lilly said. "Is she really that bad?"

"Think of the worst it could be, then multiply it by ten," Archie said bitterly. "I honestly thought after we'd helped her get her name on the byline, she'd settle down and be grateful. Unfortunately, it wasn't enough to persuade the big bods she had the skills, so they didn't back her up. She's returned to doing her agony aunt column, which doesn't amount to much, and the odd human interest piece, which she's not very good at either, unfortunately. Not enough interest, sympathy or motivation for the reader. She's taken to demanding a position on the investigative journalism team, and I'm not going to put up with it anymore. She's already stolen evidence from my desk once."

"Couldn't she have been fired for that, Archie?" Stacey asked.

"At the time, yes, if I'd reported it. But there's too much water passed under the bridge now. Not to mention I let her co-write the article in the first place. I wouldn't have a leg to stand on. Has she given you any more trouble, Lilly?"

For a long time Abigail had been a thorn in Lilly's side, insisting she remove the letterbox from outside her shop as it was interfering with her job. The fact people preferred to write to Lilly had not crossed her mind, she was insistent that Lilly was doing it deliberately to make her look like a fool.

"Honestly, since the article ran, I haven't heard from her. She knows I'm the main reason she was allowed to co-write it in the first place, so I imagine that's why she's left me alone as long as she has."

"Lilly's getting a lot more agony aunt letters though," Stacey said. "Since you mentioned the letterbox in the article, Archie, people have been writing in from everywhere. There's at least three or four new letters in it every day now."

"That's true," Lilly said, nodding.

"You always were good at it. A lot better than Abigail Douglas, that's for sure."

"Thanks, Archie. Stacey, could you hand me an order form for repairs, please?" She glanced up when Stacey didn't respond. She was staring at her phone while sending a text. "Earth to Stacey!" Lilly said, a little louder, and Stacey jumped.

"Sorry, what did you need?" She asked, stuffing her phone in her pocket.

"A repair order form."

Stacey located the paperwork and handed it over. Lilly filled it in, asked Archie to sign in then sent Stacey back into the storeroom with the form and the cup. There was a designated shelf with all the repairs Lilly had to do that week. She watched as Stacey disappeared before turning to Archie.

"She's been a bit distracted lately. I think something might be going on. I might need to talk to her about it."

Archie stood up, stretching his back, then grabbed his hat from the counter and put it on. "Don't prod, Lilly. She's a student and probably doesn't want you nosing into her private business. You're already her boss and her landlord, you don't need to be a parent too."

"Yes, all right, Archie," she huffed in response. She thought back to her conversation with Dr Jorgenson. If Archie was pointing it out too, she wondered if she really was guilty of prying too much. It was difficult not to be concerned when there was something so obviously amiss.

*S*TACEY TOOK A while to return from the back room, and Lilly suspected it was because she'd been on her phone again. She elected not to mention it. Stacey had always been a highly personable and productive employee, and it shouldn't be necessary to introduce a no phone policy. It should be a given during work hours unless it was an emergency. Yet, for the past couple of days, Stacey had been glued to her phone far more than usual.

Lilly couldn't help but think that Stacey's out of character behaviour had something to do with her father's reappearance in her life. She clearly had a lot of baggage where James Pepper was concerned, and the way he'd acted when the girl had first come to England was, to Lilly's mind, downright insulting.

But then again, it was hardly her job to judge. He *had* come rushing to Plumpton Mallet when Stacey had been injured, so in his own way he did care. Lilly idly wondered if Stacey would consider moving down to the capital to be closer to her father. The thought worried her, but she shouldn't try to stop her if that's what she wanted. Her thoughts were interrupted when the shop door opened and a familiar face entered.

"Hello, Mrs Davenport, nice to see you again."

Elizabeth Davenport was a rotund woman of indeterminate age who was always dressed to the nines regardless of what her plans for the day were. She walked with a dignified elegance that spoke of socialites of a bygone era and tilted her head back as though looking down her nose at those around her. Comical looking considering her short stature.

"Miss Tweed," she said in reply. "How have you been, my dear?"

"Very well, thank you. Is there anything I can help you with?"

"Just browsing today. Your shop has been the talk of the town recently, and I'm rather ashamed to admit I haven't been in since you first opened. You've added to your inventory I see, those gift hampers are new. I'll have a good look round and perhaps will pick up a little something for myself before I leave." She concluded, before making her way to the rear of the shop to admire some of the silver tea spoons and cake slices.

Stacey, who'd returned from the back and was now standing near Lilly, whispered, "She sounds like the Queen of England."

Lilly smiled but warned Stacey to hush. Stacey grinned in response.

The shop bell tinkled once more and several well-dressed women entered together. Lilly recognised the woman in the lead immediately. She touched Stacey's shoulder and leaned over, whispering. "That's Lady Defoe. Be as professional as possible while she's here, please."

"Me? Professional? Always," Stacey replied, shoving her phone in her pocket, as though she knew she'd been anything but by being glued to it for half the day. "So, like, a real Lady? As in Lord and Lady?" she whispered.

Lilly nodded. Plumpton Mallet may be a historic market town, but it was one of the most sought after places to live in the north of the country, and counted among its residents several members of the aristocracy.

"Welcome to The Tea Emporium," Lilly said as Lady Defoe caught her eye.

The woman smiled politely. "You have a very beautiful shop."

"Thank you."

"Oh, would you look at these adorable teapots? This one is in the shape of a welsh dresser, and look at this one, tea and honey with a beehive as the lid. I've never seen anything like them. They really are exquisite." She said to her friends, who agreed unanimously.

Lilly was a wise woman. She knew if Lady Defoe made a purchase it would mark her shop as the most fashionable place to buy and consequently bring in an influx of new and very wealthy customers. She stood back, watching Lady Defoe carefully to see what piqued her interest, and waiting for an opportune moment to offer her assistance.

*L*ILLY GLANCED IN Stacey's direction and found her gawking open-mouthed at the ladies across the shop. She was utterly mesmerised by Lady Defoe's presence. She had become so adept regarding the teas and other British customs that Lilly had forgotten how alien some things still were to her. There were obviously no members of the aristocracy in the states.

"Stacey, close your mouth. We are not a codfish," Lilly said quietly, trying not to laugh.

Stacey turned and began to giggle. "Mary Poppins, right? Sorry, it's all kind of new. A real Lady. Wow!" she whispered.

"She's just a person, one with a title admittedly, but she's just the same as us. She's also someone I wouldn't mind frequenting my shop from time to time. It's bound to attract positive attention if she begins to purchase from me."

"Right, got it," Stacey said. Turning and getting on with restocking the shelves.

Lady Defoe was, as expected, perusing the high end tea sets Lilly displayed in a locked art deco style cabinet. Since opening the shop, Lilly had only sold one single item from that cabinet and it had been an individual twenty-four carat gold rimmed teacup, for a lady wanting to replace one in a set she already owned.

"Now these are sublime." Naturally, her friends all agreed with her. "I *have* been looking for a new set..."

"I can see why you wanted to come here," one of the others said. "I must tell my husband about this place when I get back to London."

As Lilly eavesdropped on the conversation, she realised Lady Defoe was hosting a number of out-of-town friends. Among them a fashion designer, and the wife of a foreign diplomat from Paris. Lilly made her way over and smiling politely asked if there was anything she could help them with?

"I do so love this set," Lady Defoe replied, indicating the set in the cabinet. "Though I'm looking for something not quite so dark. Do you have anything similar but in a lighter shade?"

"Not in stock, but I do have an extensive catalogue you can look through. Perhaps something in there will catch your eye?"

Lady Defoe agreed and followed Lilly back to the counter. The other ladies electing to continue browsing.

"Lilith, look at these napkin rings." One lady exclaimed.

"These silver teaspoons are precious…"

"This is a beautiful linen tablecloth. Just look at the thread count."

Lady Defoe settled on one of the stools at the counter, taking in the array of fine teas displayed in the cabinet on the back wall.

"Would you like to sample one of our teas, ma'am?" Stacey asked.

Lady Defoe raised an eyebrow. "Oh, you're an American. How delightful. Where are you from?"

"Well, my mom's work meant we travelled a lot, but I spent a good bit of time in Georgia."

"I just love the southern united states. I visited Key West last year. Do you know it?"

"I do, actually. Mom and me vacationed there a lot when we were in Georgia. The last time I visited the Earnest Hemingway house."

"Oh!" Exclaimed Lady Defoe, clasping her hands together in delight. "I adore the Hemingway House. Do you know, I tried to adopt one of the polydactyl cats that live there but they wouldn't let me." She laughed. "They were offended I'd had the cheek to ask, but there were so many and so adorable, I thought they wouldn't miss one if I made a donation to the museum, but no. They wouldn't countenance the idea."

"I know, right?" Stacey said, laughing along with her. "They're the cutest things. After the tour, I sat in the garden and one hopped right in my lap and fell asleep. I wound up hanging around for ages because I didn't want to disturb it. So I sat and read *Old Man and the Sea* while one of Hemingway's cats slept in my lap."

"How romantic," Lady Defoe said before turning to Lilly with a smile. "I like this girl. Very cultured. Wherever did you find a young American who knows her teas?"

"As a matter of fact, she found me and she picked up the knowledge very quickly."

"I'll brew you up something," Stacey suggested.

"Your favourite, my dear," Lady Defoe insisted, and Stacey beamed in response, reaching for the chamomile.

Then the genial, relaxed atmosphere was spoiled.

"*L*ADY DEFOE!" MRS Davenport shrilled as she materialised out of nowhere to stand at her side. "Always such a pleasure," she continued, almost performing a curtsy.

Lilly couldn't help but notice Lady Defoe cringe briefly before relaxing her face into a polite smile. She was the epitome of good breeding and manners.

"Hello, Elizabeth. It's been a while. What brings you here?"

"The same as you, it seems. I'm looking for a new tea set."

Lilly busied herself with arranging the new gift hampers on the counter, fully aware of the reason for Mrs Davenport's change of mind. She'd gone from just browsing and possibly picking up something small to now wanting something extravagant and costly. There were no prizes for guessing why.

Stacey had finished brewing the tea and poured out for both ladies into bone china teacups with a background of vibrant green, on which were decorated an array of colourful spring flowers. Lady Defoe paused to examine and admire the china. "How pretty," she said with a smile. Everything in the shop seemed to impress the woman. Clearly, she felt as though she'd found a hidden jewel in Lilly's shop.

"Oh, I agree. Lovely colours." Mrs Davenport said, taking a sip.

"This tea is wonderful," Lady Defoe said.

"Oh, it is," Mrs Davenport agreed. "You have excellent taste, Lady Defoe."

"Oh, it wasn't my choice, Elizabeth. This young lady picked it out for me, and I'm most definitely going to need a box or two to go along with my new set." She pointed to a photograph in the catalogue, tapping the image twice for emphasis, and Lilly promptly found an order form.

It was an exquisite set, with a background of pale duck egg blue, decorated with Camellia blossoms in the palest pink, called Fairy Blush. A stunning bluebird completed the design, and it was all set off with a 24 carat gold rim around the edges of every individual piece. With a full set for six people, including side plates, teaspoons and infusers, it was the best single sale Lilly had ever had. Lady Defoe also insisted on paying in full there and then rather than just the normal deposit.

The other women also made their way to the till, each of them carrying something to purchase. They all had wide smiles and had obviously thoroughly enjoyed their shopping experience. The French diplomat's wife had bought a couple of single teacups to go with her eclectic set of mismatched ones, along with a silver-plated heart shaped infuser. The fashion designer had bought the linen tablecloth, matching napkins, and a set of six silver napkin rings. The others had selected various items, including two teapots, three gift hampers and sets of fine teaspoons.

"Mark my words, ladies," Lady Defoe said, rising from her seat. "This adorable shop is going to become a true staple of Plumpton Mallet."

Chapter Three

MRS DAVENPORT, WHO had been standing at the counter browsing the catalogue, cleared her throat. "I think I would like to order this tea set, here," she said, pointing to the exact one Lady Defoe had just bought.

"I see you and Lady Defoe have similar taste," Lilly said diplomatically. "Let me get an order form."

"Thank you, dear. It's a beautiful set, similar to the one in your cabinet I noticed, but I do love the design of this one just that bit more."

As Lilly was completing the form, the bell rang and glancing up she saw it was Fred Warren, a face she'd not seen for a while. He was a student at the local university who'd come into the shop for advice, just as the Carol Ann Hotch case began to pick up speed. He'd saved her a couple of times during that investigation.

"Fred, what a pleasure."

"Hi, Miss Tweed."

"Hey, Fred!" Stacey exclaimed enthusiastically.

Fred smiled and held up a paper bag. "I've got your lunch."

"You're the best. Thanks!"

"You can take your lunch break if you want, Stacey."

"Thanks, Lilly."

Lilly watched as Stacey and Fred made their way to the back storeroom kitchen where there was a table and chairs for breaks.

"Well, well, well..." Lilly muttered to herself. Could that explain the change in Stacey and her obsession with her phone recently? Were she and Fred dating? If they were, then Lilly was pleased for them, they made a nice couple.

"Is everything all right, dear?" asked Mrs Davenport.

"My apologies, Mrs Davenport. Yes, everything's fine. I'll put your order in this evening. Would like to pay in full or just the deposit?"

"Oh, in full is fine."

Lilly took her gold card and rang it through. Mrs Davenport may not be a member of the aristocracy but she was certainly on a par wealth wise.

"Now, Lilly. I hope you don't mind, but I have a proposition to put to you."

Lilly poured them both a cup of newly made Green Tea with Jasmine and asked Mrs Davenport what she had mind?

"Well, dear, as you are probably aware, I run one of the most popular book clubs in Plumpton Mallet." Lilly had had no idea, but she nodded anyway. "Well, our current read is a magnificent saga about a family owned tea plantation in

Africa. A beautiful, evocative story, and I happen to be the host this week."

Lilly continued to nod, patiently waiting for Mrs Davenport to get to the point, because she had no idea where all this seemingly irrelevant information was heading.

"Now, from what I hear on the grapevine, you know your teas very well."

"Yes, I do. I've always had an interest and had gained a vast knowledge even before opening The Tea Emporium. It was a natural transition for me to make after I left the paper."

"Well, Lilly, I would like you to come along and give the book club a talk on your teas and a demonstration of how to make a perfect cup using your various samples. You've become rather famous around here, haven't you?" she added, revealing her true motivation. "So, how does that sound?"

Lilly sipped her tea while she thought. Mrs Davenport had a reputation for being a bit pretentious and a bit of a snob. She liked to surround herself with important people, and it was apparent that Lilly had garnered her attention thanks to her sudden rise in popularity as a sleuth. A part of Lilly didn't want to be used in such a way, but on the other hand she recognised what a good opportunity it would be for her business. It would be foolhardy of her to bite her nose off to spite her face.

"It sounds very interesting, Mrs Davenport, although I've not done anything like that before, so don't have a fee off the top of my head."

"A fee?"

Lilly realised the woman had expected her to do it for free, no doubt for the supposed PR benefit.

"Well, if you're wanting your group to be able to sample the teas, then it will cost me in merchandise. Not to mention my time in preparing and presenting, which will take me away from my business."

"I see," Mrs Davenport said, looking crestfallen.

"How many are in your book club?"

"Usually, we have at least five or six in attendance."

Lilly thought for a moment, then nodded as she worked out a suitable compromise.

"How about seventy-five pounds for the fee? but I'll bring along a selection of my merchandise to sell. If I do well and manage to sell a few items and it's enough to cover the fee, then I will waive it completely. I will take care of everything. All you'll need to do is inform your members they'll need cash deposits if they wish to buy anything, but receipts will be given. How does that sound?"

"Oh yes, that's much more agreeable." Mrs Davenport said, suitably buoyed again.

"Wonderful, here's my business card. You can send me all the details and I'll be sure to prepare a good presentation for you and your club members."

"Thank you, my dear. I do believe my guests will enjoy it very much. After all, your shop is truly on its way to becoming a town staple." With that regurgitation of Lady Defoe's parting words, Elizabeth Davenport sailed out of the shop like a tug boat.

"OH, I JUST love the sets you've picked out for this!" Stacey declared as she helped pack the merchandise that would be part of the first outside event Lilly had done.

"Thanks, Stacey. I wanted to make sure I had something for every budget," Lilly said, passing her a dusky pink coloured teacup with a single dark pink rose and turquoise leaf design. It was part of the vintage range and one of her favourites. Lilly had planned everything down to the last second and was determined to provide an entertaining and interesting presentation for the ladies Elizabeth Davenport was hosting at her book club.

"Do you think there will be a lot of important people there?" Stacey asked. She'd certainly lived up to her name this week, as she'd peppered Lilly with questions about the Defoe family non stop ever since the family matriarch had visited the shop. She was interested in learning more about British history and culture since it was a strong part of her identity despite having grown up the states.

"Not a lot, there's usually only half a dozen or so apparently, but knowing Mrs Davenport they will certainly be influential I should think."

Lilly passed Stacey several tea infusers and a set of teaspoons with ceramic Alice in Wonderland decorated, handles. "I'm quite sure she only invited me because Lady Defoe complimented my shop and due to my newfound fame as a sleuth. Ridiculous as that is."

"Seems a bit shallow," Stacey said.

"I suppose it could be conceived that way, it's all about social games though, isn't it? It's common the world over, not just in rural England. I mean, you only need to look at the news and social media to see it in action."

"Yeah, I suppose you're right. It's a bit sad though, right?" Lilly nodded.

"Well, I've got the shop today. Earl will help me hold down the fort."

Earl meowed from the doorway when he heard his name, he'd been watching proceedings with an avid interest. Probably wondering when he could commandeer an empty box. "We're still here, Mr Grey," Lilly said, scratching his ears, before taking the last of the boxes out the back door to her car.

Before she left, she returned to double check the till float and saw Stacey was once again glued to her phone, a giddy smile plastered across her face.

"You know, Stacey," she said gently. "I really like Fred, and I'm glad you've become friends. But, I'd appreciate it if the phone stayed in your pocket during working hours."

Stacey's face went scarlet. "Oh," she said. "Um... of course. I'm sorry, we're not..."

"You don't have to tell me, Stacey, it's none of my business. But I do know how exciting the beginnings of a relationship are, I've been there myself. The odd text is fine providing it doesn't affect productivity."

"Thanks, Lilly," she said with a weak smile.

The worried expression caused Lilly to pause. "Is there something else worrying you?"

Stacey put her phone in her pocket and sighed. "Fred wants to introduce me to his family."

"Does he? Well, I'd say that's a very good sign. But it's not something you're ready for, is that it?"

"No, I'm totally fine with meeting his family, it's just I haven't told him about my family drama. You know, with my dad. I'm a bit embarrassed, if I'm honest."

"Stacey, everyone has family drama of one sort or another, it's nothing to be embarrassed about. Your experience is a lot more common than you'd think, and I'm sure Fred would understand if you explained it to him. He's a sensible young man with a good head in his shoulders."

"Yeah, it's just that things with my dad are so strange right now, and bringing a boyfriend into the picture, well it would be nice to be able to keep those things separate for a while, you know?"

"I do know. And if you explain it to Fred, I'm sure he will too," Lilly assured her.

"Thanks, Lilly."

'No problem. If you want to talk, Stacey, I'm happy to listen," she said, checking the till as she'd intended to before she left. "But for now, I really need to go if I'm to make this book club meeting on time."

*E*LIZABETH DAVENPORT HAD given Lilly comprehensive directions to her house: across the bridge that went over the tunnel she rode through into the park, when she took her bike to work. Continue up the road until it reaches the top of the woods and then take a left. Her house, a very large detached in an acre of grounds, was the second on the left. Named Dovecote Grange.

The weather was glorious, very hot with brilliant sunshine in a sky of bright blue. Not a cloud in sight. Elizabeth had told her the book club would be meeting in the garden, under the rose covered pergola, and Lilly could set up in the garden room. A glass covered orangerie style area with wicker seating, brightly coloured soft furnishings and a huge array of plants. Lilly thought it sounded perfect. The demonstration would be at a seating area on the outdoor patio area, alfresco style.

As she pulled up outside, the double wrought-iron gates opened automatically, and once Lilly was through, closed behind her. She continued down the gravel drive, flanked with blossoming rose bushes, Dahlia and marigolds, until she reached the front of the house. Elizabeth Davenport was there to meet her.

"Ah, Lilly, perfect timing. Are you excited to present?"

"Do you know? I am, as a matter of fact. Thank you for the opportunity, Elizabeth," Lilly replied with a smile.

"I'll show you where you can set up. Follow me."

Lilly was led through the hallway to the rear of the house and into the garden room. The back of the house was as beautiful as the front, with a well landscaped garden consisting of verdant lawns, established trees and colourful beds. Set in the distance were several ornate white dovecotes, which obviously gave the house its name. In the room itself, against one wall, a sideboard was available for her to display her wares and next to that a table adjacent to the wall outlets for the kettles. Water, Elizabeth said, could be obtained from the kitchen inside to the left.

"And I thought," she said, taking Lilly out onto the terrace. "That this is where we could sit while you're serving the tea and explaining their benefits."

It was a large wrought-iron chair and table set in white, adorned with red, white and blue striped cushions, very French looking and perfect for the occasion. There was also a huge free-standing garden umbrella in royal blue for much needed shade.

"I also have a table cloth should you need one?"

"This is lovely, Elizabeth, thank you. I have brought my own cloths. A pale blue with a yellow and white embroidered daisy design for out here, I thought?"

"Oh, how perfectly summer!" she exclaimed, glancing at the small, neat gold watch on her wrist. "Now, my guests will be arriving shortly and will most likely walk straight through the house to the pergola, over there. We'll keep it short and sweet this week so you'll probably have three quarters of an hour or so to get ready before your presentation."

"That should be plenty of time. I'll just go and get what I need from the car."

"Wonderful. You can use the gate at the side of the house, it will save you having to walk through. Now if you'll excuse me, I have biscuits in the oven to serve with the tea."

Lilly smiled as Mrs Davenport scurried back inside. She was absolutely in her element playing hostess. It took Lilly six trips back and forth to get everything she needed, and twenty minutes later the display inside the garden room was complete. She'd added vases of faux greenery and artificial but very realistic tea roses in creams and pinks, then finalised it all with sprinkles of rose petals. She was very pleased with the end result. And when Mrs Davenport entered, so was she.

ℭℯℓℯ𝒟

"OH, LILLY, HOW gorgeous. You've clearly put a great deal of work and imagination into this," she said. "It looks like something the Savoy or Claridges would do.

Lilly turned and smiled, seeing her host now had a guest in tow.

"Lilly, let me introduce you to Jane Nolan," Mrs Davenport began, indicating the woman who had already moved away to examine Elizabeth's orchids. She turned to Lilly and said in hushed tones, "Jane's just inherited two of Plumpton Mallet's best hotels and a number of other properties around the town from her father." She dropped to a lower whisper. "She's now one of the richest single women in town to come from new money. Her family is all new money, you see, but they've made quite a splash, nonetheless." She turned to Jane. "Jane, dear, this is Lillian Tweed. She owns that precious new tea shop in the market square."

Lilly nodded politely.

"How do you do?" Jane said, without meeting Lilly's gaze. She had what Lilly recognised as a supercilious hauteur. Very aloof and unfriendly, as though Lilly were so far beneath her she mattered very little. She wandered over to the display table as a tea set caught her eye.

"How pretty. I've not seen one quite like this before."

It was the darkest blue one with gold accents, not a rare colour scheme, it was the peacock design that made it unusual. Lilly was about to give her more information on the artist, when Jane excused herself and wandered out into the garden. Lilly frowned, hoping she wasn't going to be treated like 'trade' by all of Elizabeth's guests just because she hadn't been born into wealth and privilege.

"I'll come with you, Jane," Mrs Davenport called out, then quickly turned back to Lilly. "If Lady Defoe arrives, would you mind calling me?"

"Of course, I didn't realise she would be coming."

"Well, I naturally invited her and explained you would be attendance to do a bespoke presentation. I didn't hear back, but of course she's very busy."

Lilly nodded. She doubted Lady Defoe would turn up, but privately wondered if half the reason she'd been invited in the first place was to see if it would be enough to lure the biggest fish. There was no doubt it would be a coup for Elizabeth Davenport to have a woman of her standing attend her little function.

When Elizabeth had gone, Lilly started on the table outside. It was a meticulous process setting up an elegant table, but Lilly knew the type of women who were attending would expect the fine details. Not only that, they would also be able to identify immediately if anything was out of place. She was just placing the sugar bowl and tongs on the central tray when she heard a familiar voice, "Lillian Tweed."

Lilly couldn't believe it, it was none other than Abigail Douglas.

Chapter Four

BIGAIL DID NOT look pleased at Lilly's presence. Lilly had thought the two of them were on better terms, but the glower of hostility suggested otherwise. She really hoped Abigail wasn't going to ruin the day.

"What are you doing here?" she demanded. "Please, don't tell me you've joined Elizabeth's book club?"

"No, I haven't joined the book club. But you could sound a little more grateful, Abigail."

"Grateful? What on earth should I be grateful for?"

Lilly was aghast. "Are you serious? What's wrong with you?"

After Lilly had stopped her getting arrested and then helped her get the job to write the biggest headline article the area had seen, she thought this antagonistic attitude would be dropped. Unfortunately, it seemed as though things were worse than before. She was now beginning to think the little note of thanks Abigail had scrawled on the newspaper and dropped in Lilly's letterbox, had been written because she'd been told to, rather than because she was genuinely thankful for Lilly's help.

"I don't know, Lilly, maybe it's because your agony aunt box has turned my job into a complete joke."

"Oh, will you please change the record, Abigail? I thought you'd got over that."

"I'm still the paper's agony aunt," Abigail hissed. "And my column took yet another blow after that article came out."

Lilly very nearly laughed. *Oh, the irony,* she thought. *She wrote that article herself.*

"You think it's funny," Abigail snapped. "You are so childish."

"I don't really think it's funny, but you've only got yourself to blame, Abigail. You were the one who wrote the article, so you can't blame me for the situation you find yourself in. You should try giving better advice if your column isn't doing well. And that's a free bit of advice from the gazette's most popular agony aunt."

Abigail's jaw fell open. "I... well, how utterly rude!" she spluttered and stormed off across the lawn towards the pergola.

With the tables complete, Lilly took her two kettles to the kitchen to fill. As she returned, she noticed a new face had joined Elizabeth, Jane and Abigail, it was Lady Meredith Gresham, another prominent town resident. Lilly smiled, it looked as though Elizabeth's desire to have a member of the aristocracy in her circle had been answered.

"Ooh, what a heavenly display!" A jolly and very cultured voice said behind her, causing Lilly to jump.

"Oh, hello."

"Sorry, I didn't mean to startle you," the woman said, holding out her hand. "Isadora Smith."

"Lillian Tweed, but you can call me Lilly," she said, shaking hands with the eccentrically, but beautifully dressed woman in a large straw hat. "Are you here for the book club?"

"Yes, I'm a little late, one of the dogs ran off and I couldn't find her for ages. Turned out she'd gone home by herself and was waiting at the door when I got back." She giggled.

Lilly laughed with her, then indicated the pergola where the others were waiting. Isadora tripped across the lawn to the sound of Jane Nolan's slightly sarcastic voice, "Fashionably late as always, Isadora." Lilly noticed the final guest didn't reply but shook her head slightly in annoyance.

While the women were discussing the book Lilly sat and waited in the garden room, she'd brought a book of her own to read, which made the time fly. Eventually they all started to saunter slowly back across the lawn and made their way to the outdoor table. She joined them on the terrace just as the last of them took a seat.

❦

"*L*ADIES, WELCOME," LILLY started by saying. She could tell Abigail was looking at her with unconcealed judgment, no doubt hoping she would fail miserably. "Thank you for having me here today, especially our host Elizabeth for the idea and the invitation."

There was a chorus of agreement along with a smattering of applause, and Elizabeth beamed in delight.

Lilly settled a teapot on the table and lifted the lid to give it a final stir.

"Oh, what a lovely scent," Jane said, sitting upright.

"This is lemon infused nettle tea, one of my personal favourites," Lilly began, pouring each of them a sample. "We'll be trying lots of different tea types today and I'll go through some of the health benefits of each. This nettle tea, for instance, is an excellent source of both iron and calcium. When I first opened the shop, I started to cycle into work and chose this tea because it helps to prevent leg cramping and relieves rheumatism. It can be also be flavoured with lime and honey. Having a cup each morning has helped my legs and knees no end."

"Really?" Lady Meredith asked. "So, it's potentially beneficial for those who suffer from arthritis?"

"Indeed. The joints could benefit greatly from having a regular dose of nettle tea, and it's also known to decrease blood sugar and lower blood pressure. With this tea it's better not to exceed four cups a day, that's if the tea is made from the leaves. If made from the root, then a single cup is the recommended dose."

"My mother-in-law suffers from dreadful arthritis," Lady Gresham said, taking another sip. "Perhaps I should suggest some of this for her to my husband when he returns from Asia..."

While Elizabeth Davenport handed round her biscuits, Lilly rinsed the tea cups at the table, pouring the dregs into a pansy decorated china pot made for the purpose, then returned to the garden room to brew the next sample. She'd chosen a green tea this time and after pouring continued with her lecture. As she talked and the ladies sipped, nodded and asked questions, she handed out various catalogues and leaflets, and the conversation soon turned to the tea sets she had available.

"I adore that one you have over there," Jane said, waving her arm in the general direction of the display table. "Is it available to buy?"

"Yes," Lilly confirmed. "All the items and the sets you see here today are available, including the one we're using for the samples. What's in the catalogue can be ordered specifically in whatever size you require. Mrs Davenport just ordered one recently in fact."

"Page twenty-two. What do you think, ladies?"

"It's beautiful, Elizabeth. You have such exquisite taste," Lady Gresham said.

"I agree, it's quite beautiful," said Jane. "And this demonstration was a wonderful idea."

"Yes it was," Abigail muttered, albeit reluctantly.

Lilly went back inside to get another sample, one of her finer mint teas, and returned to the table pouring for Isadora Smith first. "Oh, what a lovely hatpin."

The large sun hat Lilly had noticed when Isadora had first arrived was pinned in place by a silver pin with an ornate butterfly design.

"Thank you, Lilly. I know they are probably thought old fashioned nowadays, but I do so adore them. They speak of history and more genteel days, I feel."

"It is beautiful, Isadora," Lady Gresham said, leaning over to get a better look. "Personally, I wish the style would come back, although I'm not sure I'd be brave enough to wear them. I'm not really suited to hats except for weddings, and Ladies Day at Royal Ascot, of course."

Suddenly Mrs Davenport zeroed in on the subject. "Once Lilly has finished, Lady Gresham, I'd love to show you my collection."

Isadora frowned slightly.

"You collect hatpins, Elizabeth?" Lady Gresham asked in surprise.

"Oh, I do. I simply adore them. I have quite a few, although I imagine they're a bit older than the one Isadora is wearing."

"Antiques then?"

"That's right. Some nearly one-hundred and fifty years old."

"As is mine, Elizabeth," Isadora said, with a tight smile.

Lilly could immediately feel the tension between Elizabeth and Isadora. Mind you, a lot of people had strong feelings when it came to Elizabeth Davenport, she had a real knack for stepping on toes. Attempting to diffuse the situation before it got out of hand she spoke about the tea they were drinking. "This is one of my mint blends, excellent for calming nerves and is a wonderful choice for evening as it promotes restful sleep."

"I could use a whole pot of this before bed," Jane said, and the others laughed.

"Any other health benefits to this one?" Abigail asked.

"It's certainly one of the best teas for relieving tension headaches as well as easing digestive upsets."

"Isn't this one of the samples you gave me in your shop the other day, when we were with Lady Defoe?" Mrs Davenport said.

It wasn't but before Lilly could correct her, Jane spoke.

"Oh, you saw Lady Defoe, Elizabeth?"

"Why yes, we sampled tea together in Lilly's shop," she replied, giving Jane a snide look, which Lilly noticed. Why Mrs Davenport was friends with so many people that she seemed to have ill will towards, Lilly couldn't understand.

"I think I've found a teapot I'd like to order," Isadora said, marking the page in the catalogue.

"Wonderful, I'll get some order forms after I bring the last pot."

Lilly hurried inside to fetch the last sample of the day, a superior chamomile blend. After sampling, it proved to be a popular choice and nearly all of them ordered a box. They all bought other items too. Jane, the tea set she'd been admiring since her arrival. Lady Gresham a tea set from the catalogue as well as a box of nettle tea for her mother-in-law, and the mint for herself. Mrs Davenport chose the mint. Even Abigail bought a box of mint to go with the chamomile she'd also liked. All in all, it had been an excellent day for Lilly and Mrs Davenport's fee had been covered several times over. Perhaps she should start to provide this sort of service officially?

Although the demonstration was over, the ladies didn't seem to want to leave. They stood on the terrace talking while Lilly cleared and packed everything away. Elizabeth had brought out glasses of champagne. Jane had slipped inside a few minutes before, but the rest continued to discuss their purchases and the surprising health benefits of tea while sipping an obviously favourite tipple.

Lilly packed up carefully, but efficiently and made the several trips through the gate at the side of the house to load up her car. After she'd stowed away the last of her items, she made her way back round to the terrace to say her final goodbye.

Elizabeth, Abigail and Isadora were the only ones left on the terrace when she returned. "Ladies, I just want to say thank you again for having me," Lilly began, but before any of them could respond they heard a terrified scream from inside the house.

*T*HE SCREAM HAD been ghastly and sent all four of them dashing inside in time to see a ghostly looking Lady Gresham running towards them from inside the house. She let out a second shriek, almost colliding with Elizabeth Davenport as she reached out to her, grasping her shoulders. "Elizabeth," Meredith cried, tears streaking down her face. "It's Jane. In the powder room."

"Jane? What about Jane, Meredith?"

"She's hurt. There's blood. So much blood!"

"Call the police," Lilly shouted as she ran to the cloakroom. She flung open the door to find Jane Nolan lying on the floor, eyes closed and head resting in a small pool of blood. "Jane!" Lilly exclaimed, getting down on her knees next to the prone woman. Her lips were pale and Lilly quickly located a deep cut near her throat. Jane's hands were covered in blood, and Lilly imagined she'd tried to stem the flow before passing out. She lifted a wrist and attempted to locate a pulse. There wasn't one. "Oh, Jane..." she said, getting up in shock and looking away.

Her eyes fell on the white sink where a small pool of water sat in the basin, stained a pale pink as though someone had just washed their hands. Surely Lady Gresham hadn't paused to wash her hands before raising the alarm?

Lilly hurried out of the room where she was met with a sea of frightened faces. Isadora was on her mobile with the emergency services. "They want to know if she's breathing?" she asked Lilly, glancing behind her into the room, eyes widening in shock at the grotesque scene.

Lilly shook her head. "No, she's not breathing. I felt for a pulse. I'm terribly sorry, but I'm afraid she's dead."

Isadora stepped away from the others and repeated the grave news to the operator.

"I don't understand," Elizabeth stuttered. "What happened?"

"I don't know," Lilly said. "But there's a neck injury and quite a lot of blood."

Lilly saw Abigail fiddling with her phone and realised, unbelievably, that she was trying to take a sneaky photograph of the scene. She stepped in front of the door and snarled at her, "Have some decency, Abigail. Don't embarrass yourself." Abigail promptly put her phone away and disappeared from view. Lilly turned to the others, shutting the cloakroom door to try to give Jane at least some dignity in death and suggested they all move back to the garden room or the terrace and wait for the police. There was nothing more they could do. Jane Nolan was beyond help.

❦

*T*HE DOORBELL RANG not long afterwards, and Elizabeth Davenport went to answer it. She returned with three police officers, one of whom was Sergeant Bonnie Phillips, an old friend of Lilly's. She'd known her since her old days at the gazette, having been introduced by Archie. Bonnie was Archie's contact at the station and fed him bits of information as and when she could.

The first thing Lilly noticed when she walked over to greet her friend was that she wasn't in uniform. "Plain clothes today, Bonnie?"

Bonnie smiled. "I did tell you I was moving to detective work. I've got my exams coming up shortly. So what are you doing here?" taking in the other women sitting in silent shock in the garden room.

Lilly explained briefly the reason for her presence, then the more important information about Jane Nolan's death. Bonnie sent the other two officers to assess the scene while she stayed with Lilly.

"So who found her?"

Lilly pointed to a very pale Lady Gresham. "Lady Gresham did. She screamed, and we all came rushing in from the terrace. She was on the verge of passing out due to the shock."

Bonnie nodded and made her way out to the small group. Lilly followed and took a seat in one of the spare wicker chairs.

"I don't understand," Lady Gresham was saying, wringing her hands. "How did it happen? Did she fall?"

"I'll get you some water, Meredith," Mrs Davenport said, rising to get a pitcher and some glasses from the kitchen.

Bonnie watched her as she went, and could see one of her officers had stopped her briefly to ask some questions. Abigail also stood, looking as though she was about to follow but was prevented with a severe look from Bonnie who was positioned in the doorway. Bonnie beckoned her over and they spoke in hushed tones for several minutes, while Bonnie took notes.

Lilly rubbed her eyes as she felt a headache coming on. She could hardly believe something like this could have happened. She tried to picture the cloakroom to see if she could work out what Jane had hurt herself on. There didn't seem to be anything present that would cause the injury she'd seen. Then a horrifying thought occurred to her. What if someone else had hurt Jane? But that would mean... oh no! Please not another murder in Plumpton Mallet.

Chapter Five

*L*ILLY SHIVERED AT the dreadful thought, but glancing over to where Abigail was still deep in conversation with Bonnie, she realised she wasn't the only one thinking in this way. It was why Abigail had tried to photograph the scene; she saw the story of a possible murder laid out before her and, for once, she had beaten Archie Brown to the scoop. Bonnie too, with the way she was studying each of the women in turn, was clearly looking for a suspect among them, wondering at possible motives and plausible, but faked shock and remorse. Lilly eyed the women present, but all of them looked to be as shocked and stunned as she was.

"Lilly, can I speak with you now, please?" Bonnie asked as she escorted Abigail back to her chair.

"Yes, of course," she said, rising. She passed Elizabeth, who was returning with a tray of iced water for her guests, especially Lady Gresham who was looking worse by the minute.

"Elizabeth, might I suggest hot sweet tea for Lady Gresham?" Lilly said quietly. "It's very good for shock."

"Oh, yes. What a good idea, Lilly. I'll see to that shortly."

Lilly, along with Bonnie and another officer, stood just inside the kitchen out of hearing range of the other women. "Is everything okay?" Lilly asked, then realised instantly what a stupid question it was. "Sorry, I don't mean okay, of course it isn't. I just mean..." she sighed. "What can I do to help?"

"Lilly, Constable Steel here, has just been speaking with Mrs Davenport, and as you know I've just had a chat with Abigail. We're trying to pinpoint the time of death and sequence of events as they happened. How long would you say Jane Nolan was away from you all in the cloakroom?" Bonnie asked, notebook in hand.

Lilly frowned in concentration. Now she thought about it, Jane had been gone for quite a while. "Let me see... she headed inside right after she filled in an order form for a tea set she wanted... oh, she gave me a cash deposit for it, Bonnie. I have no idea who to return that to?"

"You can give it to me, Lilly. I'll give you a receipt for it. Go on."

"Okay, thanks. The others also took a few minutes to fill out their order forms. They then finished off their tea, which took another few minutes.

"And Abigail said she went inside briefly to wash her hands?"

Lilly nodded. "Yes, I think that's right. Once everyone had finished, they moved to the terrace, freeing up the table so I could clear away. Elizabeth Davenport returned to the kitchen with her tray of biscuits. She was gone for a minute or two as well. She must have returned with champagne at some point as they were drinking that when I came out from the garden room to start clearing the table."

Constable Steel nodded, also taking notes. "Right, and then?"

Lilly thought for a moment longer. "I started packing everything up at that point. Mrs Davenport came back, that might be when she brought the champagne out come to think of it. Isadora went inside and kindly collected one of my teapots from the kitchen where she'd taken it and rinsed it out."

"Would you say everyone was inside for at least a few minutes by themselves prior to Lady Gresham finding Jane?" Bonnie asked.

Lilly frowned. "Yes, I suppose that's true."

"All except you, it seems, though you were walking back and forth down the side of the house loading up, Mrs Davenport informs us," Constable Steel said. "She commented you were working so quickly she doubted you had time to go inside."

Thank you, Elizabeth, Lilly thought, realising the woman's statement was the only reason she wasn't being treated as a suspect. "So, just so I'm clear, Bonnie, are you saying one of these women deliberately hurt Jane?"

Constable Steel and Bonnie exchanged a brief glance. "You go ahead, Steel, the pathologist, and the ambulance will be arriving shortly. Best if you meet them at the front." Bonnie said, and he left, moving to the front of the house near the cloakroom, leaving the two of them alone in the kitchen. Bonnie sighed. "This isn't good, Lilly."

"I know. What did you find? It's obvious to everyone here you're treating this as a murder inquiry."

"I'm not sure exactly, but her carotid artery was severed," Bonnie said. "She lost consciousness within a minute or two, I would think, then bled to death."

"Oh, Bonnie, that's awful," Lilly said, her hand instinctively reaching up to her neck. "What sort of weapon was used?"

"I don't know, we're looking for a possible murder weapon now, but this sort of attack should have resulted in blood splatter, and looking at all these women there's no blood on any of them."

"There was blood in the sink, I think," Lilly said. "I caught a glimpse of it when I went to see if Jane was breathing. It looked like someone had washed their hands."

Bonnie nodded. "Yes, we noticed that too. I'm guessing whoever it was came up behind her and reached round, otherwise they would have had a hard time avoiding getting blood on their clothing. It was quick and efficient, Lilly. We spoke to Elizabeth Davenport and apart from the guests at the book club there was no one else here. I asked about security, but she says there's only a house alarm, which was obviously switched off. Do you know if there was anyone else here?"

"I agree with Elizabeth. There wasn't anyone else here at all apart from us, Bonnie."

Bonnie sighed in frustration. "This is going to get nasty quickly, Lilly. Not only was Jane Nolan a prominent and very wealthy citizen, but she was found by Lady Gresham. People are going to be all over this, the press especially. Abigail being here is only going to make matters worse. We need to solve this crime quickly before people start to speculate about what happened. There's no doubt about it, Lilly, there were a number of very important people here today, and now one of them is dead under extremely suspicious circumstances.

❦

*L*ILLY WAS RELIEVED when Bonnie told her she could leave. She'd already packed everything up before the police had arrived and had been itching to go for a while. She couldn't believe she was caught up in yet another suspicious death so soon after the previous one. There was naturally a terrible feeling of dread in the air, but unbelievably alongside that were undertones of glee and gossip which made Lilly feel nauseated. They were all distraught over Jane, of course, but there was a suggestion of thrills, almost as if they couldn't wait to tell others about what had happened in order to give themselves a sense of importance. No doubt they would be dining out on this macabre story at social functions for years to come. Lilly didn't want to be a part of it, and had an almost frantic need to distance herself from all of them.

She exited via the path at the side of the house and pulling on the door handle of her car, found it was locked. Reaching into her pockets for her keys, she frowned when they weren't there. "Oh, no," she muttered, peering in through the window to make sure she hadn't left them in the ignition or on the seat and locked herself out. She had an annoying habit of losing her car keys. She should put them on a chain around her neck or something.

"Miss Tweed! I say, Miss Tweed. Lilly!" Isadora Smith called from behind her, one hand holding her hat, the other lifting the voluminous skirt of her ankle length tea dress, as she tripped daintily down the steps like a princess coming to greet her subjects.

"Isadora," Lilly said with a smile. "Can I help with something?"

"I think you dropped these out on the terrace," she said, dangling a set of car keys. "They are yours, aren't they?"

"Oh, yes," she said, relieved she wasn't going to have to go searching for them. "I was just wondering if I'd managed to lock myself out of my car. Thanks so much. I didn't really want to go back to the terrace to look for them."

"Of course," Isadora said, dropping the keys in Lilly's outstretched hand. "Are you all right? I imagine you're terribly flustered considering what's happened, aren't you?"

Lilly was momentarily surprised that Isadora had bothered to ask, not that she'd pegged her as being self-absorbed, but Lilly herself wasn't part of this group's circle, didn't know any of them in fact apart from Abigail. She hadn't expected anyone to wonder how she was feeling.

"I'm a little shaky, but okay. I didn't know Jane personally but am very upset for her. Such a tragic thing to have happened, I can't quite believe it."

"I imagine this was not how you envisaged today ending," Isadora said with a dramatic sigh. "None of us did. I mean, how could we possibly? It's ghastly. Utterly ghastly. But, just so you know, I was very impressed with your demonstration and knowledge. I hope you won't let this awful experience deter you from doing similar events in the future? It would be such a shame if you didn't continue."

"Thank you, Isadora, I was just wondering about that exact thing."

"Really, you mustn't mind too much if you feel a little put out at all your hard work ending in such an awful way. Don't berate yourself for being upset for *you*; it's your livelihood after all."

Lilly was surprised at how astute Isadora was, she'd been feeling guilty and selfish as those very thoughts had flitted across her mind. Her ruined day couldn't compare to the loss of Jane's life.

"How are you, Isadora? Obviously you knew Jane much better than I did."

Isadora nodded. "I think I'm still in shock. It's as though I'm watching a film or a play as opposed to actually being part of it. It's a very odd feeling. I must admit, I was surprised to see Jane here when I arrived, though."

"Surprised?" Lilly asked, fiddling with her keys. She was torn between wanting to leave and wanting to hear what Isadora had to say. "Why was that?"

Isadora sighed melodramatically. "Well, I don't want to tell tales out of school as it were, but she and Elizabeth were not on the best of terms I'm afraid."

This was news to Lilly. She had picked up on the fact that Elizabeth Davenport had butted heads in one way or another with most of the women in her group, but she hadn't noticed any particular animosity towards Jane Nolan. "Why? Had something happened?"

Isadora shrugged, as though the incident wasn't really of significance. "Jane had rather a tactless way with her at times. She embarrassed Elizabeth terribly in front of Lady Defoe recently."

Lilly cast her mind back to that day in her tea shop. Mrs Davenport made no secret of the fact she wanted to be in Lady Defoe's good graces. She'd almost curtsied and her manner had been overly obsequious. She couldn't imagine how she'd react to being made to look a fool in front of her.

"Oh, dear. What happened?"

"It was at a lawn party Lady Defoe held for Easter a few months ago. A lavish affair naturally, as all her soirees are, and Elizabeth was trailing around after her like a little puppy, as she does. I'm afraid she was being a bit of a bother actually, as well as leaving her poor husband to entertain himself. Jane caught on to Lady Defoe's annoyance and accused Elizabeth of being, in veiled terms, but the implication was there for everyone to hear, a desperate little social climber. I witnessed the whole exchange, and truly, Lilly, it was mortifying for all of us, but especially for Elizabeth. Lady Defoe, gracious as ever, gently admonished Jane for her harsh tongue, but we all saw the amusement for a split second in her face. It was quite dreadful for poor Elizabeth."

"I can imagine," Lilly said. "What an awful experience that must have been for her."

"Oh, it was. She really took it to heart, poor thing. Our book club took a hiatus as a result," Isadora explained. "Today was our first meeting since Easter because no one wanted to bring Elizabeth and Jane together. We all made excuses for not hosting, but eventually Elizabeth reached out to us to start it back up again. I had assumed she simply would omit Jane, but I obviously thought too little of my friend, it seems. She did invite her and treated her perfectly well. I thought that was very brave and courteous of her."

Lilly nodded. "Yes, I'd have to agree. When Jane first arrived, Elizabeth was very kind and introduced us. I never would have guessed they were on poor terms."

"No, of course not, reputation is everything you see. But it was very accommodating of Elizabeth, nonetheless. Jane, in her usual undiplomatic way, was trying to give Lady Defoe some space, I think. It worked, but it was very poorly done, and Lady Defoe values good manners above all else. While she did momentarily let slip her amusement, she certainly wouldn't put up with one of her guests insulting another. She handled it well, I thought."

"I'm sorry to hear Elizabeth has had such a difficult time with some of her friends lately," Lilly said.

"Don't feel too sorry for her, Lilly. Elizabeth makes a rod for her own back. She and I have been known to come to verbal blows occasionally; it wasn't just a problem with her and Jane. Although we don't hold grudges. Anyway, I probably should be getting back; Lady Gresham was looking very pale when I left. I really should check on her, too."

Lilly thanked her again for returning her keys then got in the car ready to leave. As the engine roared into life, she looked up to find Abigail Douglas standing in her way.

"OH, FOR CRYING out loud," Lilly muttered, winding down her window and leaning out. "Abigail, what on earth are you doing? Get out of my way I want to leave." She noticed Abigail had a notebook under her arm and a pen in her hand.

She walked to the driver's side window and leaned in, glaring at her. "I wanted to make it clear that I would be handling this investigation, and your assistance this time will not be needed."

"You are not a police officer, Abigail," Lilly said wearily. She really was fed up now and wanted to go home.

"And neither are you," she hissed back. "I'm an investigative journalist, unlike you."

"No, you're not. You're an agony aunt."

Abigail's nostrils flared and her face turned an ugly shade of scarlet. She pointed a finger at Lilly, wagging it as she spoke. "I am a reporter. I work for the paper. You own a teashop. This does not concern you, Lillian Tweed, and I insist this time that you leave it to the professionals. Your head has become far too big since that last article, but you have absolutely no reason to be involved. Stay out of it."

Lilly rolled her eyes. Her patience with Abigail was wearing dangerously thin, but she just didn't have the energy to argue with her. "Whatever you say, Abigail. Now get out of my way otherwise I promise, I'll run you down."

Abigail's jaw fell open, but she moved so Lilly could drive out. Lilly glanced in her rear-view mirror while she waited for the gates to open. She could clearly see Abigail staring at her. *She is definitely a sandwich short of a picnic,* Lilly thought as she made her way back to town.

As she drove, her mind involuntarily turned to the image of Jane Nolan's body lying dead on the floor of the cloakroom. It was a picture she wouldn't be able to forget for a long while. The previous case she'd been involved with, the death of Carol Ann Hotch, she'd learned about second hand so hadn't seen the body at all. This time, not only had she been there when it happened, but she was a witness and had been the one to check for signs of life. You couldn't get much closer than that, and it was hitting her very differently.

Abigail, on the other hand, was almost feverish with excitement. An abnormal reaction for someone who'd just seen her friend killed. But not as bad as trying to photograph the scene with her phone. That was despicable and a far from normal act for anyone in their right mind to attempt. Then another, far more horrific thought occurred to her, and she had to pull over to calm down before she ran herself off the road, or worse.

Archie Brown had already let slip he thought Abigail was writing agony aunt letters to herself because no one else was. She was also frantic that her column would be done away with altogether, leaving her unemployed. And if what she had intimated during the last case was true, possibly homeless as well. Her idea of moving to crime reporting was to try to keep a job and a roof over her head.

Was Abigail so desperate to prove herself that she'd actually created a story to write? Would she really go as far as that?

Lilly wasn't so sure if she knew the answer.

Chapter Six

*L*ILLY TRIED HARD to forget the incident at the Davenport house that night when she got home. Stacey had already closed up for the day when she'd returned briefly to drop off the items she'd taken to the demonstration, and to pick up Earl, who was fast asleep in the window.

She'd taken a long soak in the bath, then immersed herself in a book to take her mind off things, and thankfully it had worked. The whole experience had become surreal, like being in a Jane Austen novel but with murder as part of the plot. She'd not even dreamed about it, which was a great relief because she had expected a restless night.

However, she and Bonnie had made plans for lunch the next day, ostensibly to catch up. With both of them having busy lives, they hadn't managed a get together for some time, but in reality Lilly knew the main topic of conversation would be Jane Nolan's murder.

She left Stacey to man the shop and rode her bike to the cafe in the park where they'd decided to meet. Choosing to sit outside, but in a shady corner where they wouldn't be seen or overheard, they waited until a waitress brought the menus before turning to the murder.

"You're on the case full time, then?" Lilly asked, nodding at the file Bonnie had brought with her, now sitting on the table.

"I am. I've got my exams in a couple of weeks, so although I'm not fully qualified, I'm expected to pass with flying colours according to my boss. As a consequence, they've thrown me in at the deep end with this one."

"Well, they must have a tremendous amount of confidence in you, Bonnie, considering how important all the players are. Well done."

"Thanks," she said. "A cappuccino, please," she said to the waitress who'd arrived to take their drinks order.

"I'll have the same, please," Lilly said, and the server disappeared. "Are you feeling up to the challenge?"

"Absolutely. When have you ever known me to pass up a challenge? The difference with this one is that I'm the lead on the case. Before I was always working under a superior officer, so it's a bit more stressful trying to make sure I've covered and documented every stage and possible angle. And Abigail Douglas is unfortunately involved in the whole thing, so she won't leave me alone. That, I could really do without. She thinks I'm going to be her inside woman at the station."

"Doesn't she know you've been Archie's contact at the station for years?"

"Obviously not," Bonnie said. "I'll probably drop his name next time she contacts me. That ought to persuade her to leave me alone. She won't want Archie to find out she's going behind his back, I understand he's already furious with her for a number of other transgressions."

When the waitress returned with their coffee, they ordered toasted sandwiches and a side salad to share.

Lilly's eyes shifted to the file. "So, is that..."

"Don't even think about it, Lilly. As a soon to be fully qualified detective, I can't possibly let a member of the public read a file pertaining to an ongoing murder inquiry."

"What?" said Lilly, confused. "Then why did you bring it if I can't see it?"

"All I'm saying," Bonnie said, leaning closer and dropping her voice. "Is that my reputation and job are very important, I could get myself in serious trouble if anyone thought I'd showed you this file."

"Riiiight," said Lilly in exaggeration. "So, are you letting me look at it or not?"

"I'm not *letting* you do anything," Bonnie replied, casually pushing the file nearer to Lilly. "Right, I must go to the bathroom. Back in minute."

"Ah, I get it, plausible deniability," Lilly muttered to herself, snatching up the file when Bonnie had gone. It was Jane Nolan's autopsy report. It made for gruesome reading, and Lilly quickly scanned the text, then turned the loose page over to find an x-ray of Jane's head and shoulders.

"Oh wow," she breathed. There was something long and thin lodged in the side of her neck. The previous typed report sheet had said an unidentifiable metal rod, approximately two millimetres in circumference and just over ten centimetres in length, had been thrust at an angle through the windpipe and pierced the carotid artery. It stated the victim would have passed out through lack of oxygen within a minute before bleeding to death.

Lilly looked up in time to see Bonnie exiting the cafe and making her way back to their table. She grabbed her phone and took a quick picture of the x-ray before sliding the file back into place.

"So," Bonnie said, picking up the sandwich Lilly hadn't realised had arrived. "They found a length of metal in her neck."

"You don't say?" Lilly replied in sarcastic tones. Bonnie frowned and Lilly grinned. "Sorry. So what do you think it is?"

"I was hoping you could venture a guess. Anything come to mind?"

"A very thin metal rod about ten centimetres long? I honestly have no idea."

"Actually, the metal broke off in her neck," Bonnie explained. "So the murder weapon would most likely have been longer, although how much longer we can't say until we find the missing piece. I searched the immediate scene for the rest of it but came up empty. I honestly can't figure out what it is, it's even got my colleagues at the station and the morgue people scratching their heads."

"So that's why you wanted me to look at the file," Lilly said.

"I don't know anything about that," Bonnie said, and Lilly gave her a look. "I've got to be careful, Lilly. Not only could you seeing this file risk the chain of evidence, but I could lose my job. I need to be able to plead innocence if needed. So, I didn't share this with you, okay?"

"I do understand, Bonnie. You being up for promotion is complicating things."

"It's not as though I knew what you were up to last time. You never told me you were investigation the Carol Ann Hotch case. I assumed you were asking questions because she'd written to you. If I had known what you were doing, I probably would have tried to stop you.

"What about this time?" Lilly asked, curious. She hadn't made up her mind whether to pursue the question of what happened to Jane herself yet. "If I do decide to look into things, and I am not saying I will at this stage, the whole thing has left a sour taste in my mouth if I'm being honest, but if I do will you try to stop me?"

"I'll pretend I didn't hear that. I'm going to deny everything," Bonnie said. "Because you're a grown woman who is going to do what she wants anyway. I do however greatly value your opinion, Lilly, although this isn't me asking you to get involved. I just wanted to see if you had any idea what the implement in her neck was?"

"I'm afraid not. I wish I could be more help."

"Don't worry. But if you think of anything remotely plausible, can you let me know?"

"Of course I will," Lilly assured her, and they finished their lunch talking about anything and everything else but murder.

*A*FTER LUNCH WITH Bonnie, Lilly felt a bit weighed down with responsibility. While her friend hadn't made a big deal out of it, nor asked her outright, Lilly assumed that Bonnie really wanted her involvement. She obviously couldn't come right out and ask her, but the subtle hints had been there, and this was her first real case, and it was a big one. She needed to solve it and as quickly as possible. But did she need Lilly to help her do that?

The police were in a bit of a predicament. This case was a highly sensitive one with the women of the book club all being prominent, wealthy and influential residents. Every step of the process would have to be meticulously dealt with, every 't' crossed and 'i' dotted. To accuse any one of these women, they would need to have all the necessary evidence at their fingertips to back it up. Lilly didn't envy Bonnie her job, it was a political nightmare.

As she cycled back to the shop, her mind was in a whirl trying to work out what Bonnie had actually meant. *Does she want me to get involved because she knows I could ignore the red tape? Could I get myself into trouble if I start snooping around? I certainly came close last time. She kept saying she didn't want me to get involved, but the way she was acting suggested otherwise. What if I'm misreading her signals?*

By the time she got back to the shop she was no nearer working out what Bonnie really wanted and was almost tempted to ring her and ask her to come out and say it plainly one way or another. But that was a stupid idea.

She parked her bike in its usual spot, chained it to the post and put the flower baskets in place. It had become a recognised staple of the shop front display now, and she regularly found tourists posing and taking photos beside it. She tapped on the glass and Earl opened his eyes, gave a huge yawn which showed his needle-like teeth, then turned over and went back to sleep.

She grabbed the lunch she'd brought for Stacey and entered the shop, finding her pouring a sample for a male customer at the far end of the counter.

"Here's your lunch, Stacey," she said, putting the bag on the counter just as the man turned his head. It was James Pepper, Stacey's father.

"Oh, Mr Pepper, what a surprise, I didn't realise it was you."

"Miss Tweed," he said with a nod before turning back to his tea.

"Thanks, Lilly," Stacey said, turning to her father. "I'm just going to have my lunch. I'll be back down in a bit."

Stacey had got into the habit of taking her lunch upstairs to her flat, where she'd quickly do the laundry or the washing up while she ate. The young woman was pleased with the convenience of living above where she worked, and Lilly couldn't blame her. She had, for a brief moment, considered moving up there herself, but she loved her cottage too much to leave it. Besides, she really needed a garden, not just for her but for Earl.

As Stacey left out of the back door, Lilly made her way behind the counter, secretly wishing another customer would walk in so she could avoid having to have a conversation with James. For some reason, and not just because of his lax attitude towards his daughter, Lilly hadn't really taken to him. Admittedly, she didn't really know him well enough to judge him, but she couldn't shake off the way she felt.

"How was your lunch?" he asked once she was settled by the till.

"It was very nice," Lilly replied. "A perfect day to sit outside and enjoy the sunshine."

"That's always nice," he said. There was a long, increasingly awkward silence as he sipped his tea and Lilly sorted through her tea samples. Eventually to fill the void, he started to make small talk. "I'm surprised Stacey knows as much about tea as she does. Her mother certainly was never much of a tea drinker. Americans seem to think you have to drink the stuff cold and sweetened with so much sugar it would rot your teeth just by looking at it."

Lilly smiled at him. He was trying hard to make conversation. She felt a bit ashamed at her feelings towards him and was sure he could tell she wasn't a fan. Usually she prided herself on her discretion and manners. She really should make a better effort. She wondered for a moment if Dr Jorgenson was right, that her ill feeling stemmed from the possibility that she was viewing his daughter as the one she had never had, or worse that Stacey would leave. This was something she would have to work through herself. She shouldn't take it out on a man who appeared to be honestly trying to better his relationship with his daughter.

"How did the two of you meet? Stacey mentioned her mother travelled a lot."

"Yes, she was a writer. And a painter. Sometime musician and did a bit of acting, too. Even had interest in the sciences. She was a true Renaissance character. She went where the work was. We met in London at the university where I teach."

Lilly nodded. "Yes, I remember now, Stacey mentioned you were a professor. What do you teach?"

"History," he said, smiling. "I dabble in a bit of everything, but I specialise in American History. You can imagine how meeting Stacey's mother, a beautiful American artist, caught my attention. She dreamed of writing the next great American novel. The two of us actually worked together on a book for a while before we separated. It was never finished."

"I'm sorry. Do you mind me asking how Stacey ended up at university here, when the London one is so prestigious? I'm sure you could have helped her get accepted there."

The question evidently struck a nerve. James Pepper tensed up for a moment, gripping his teacup so tightly Lilly thought he might break it. When he returned it to its saucer, he let out a deep sigh.

"You don't like me very much, do you?" he said, confirming Lilly's suspicions.

"What makes you think that?" she replied, neither confirming nor denying, but feeling dreadful that she'd been so transparent.

"Look, I can tell you mean a lot to Stacey and I'm grateful you've been a source of support for her while she's so far from home. I do hope you and I can get along."

"I would prefer it."

"Then to answer your original question, I didn't want Stacey going to the school where I was teaching. I'm a bachelor, stuck in my ways I suppose, and didn't want the interruptions and change of lifestyle having a daughter nearby would mean. I avoided her phone calls when she began talking about coming to England, and I believe I hurt her. She came anyway and was accepted up here."

Lilly couldn't think of anything to say, which wasn't either barbed or sarcastic. *You should be ashamed of yourself*, and *how selfish can you get?* Were absolutely not the correct responses. As an agony aunt she should have been able to give impartial advice, but with Stacey involved she found she couldn't. She kept her mouth shut.

"I know what you're thinking," Mr Pepper continued. "I realise I've been very selfish and I'm trying to make up for my behavior. There's nothing you can say to me that I haven't already said to myself a hundred times, Miss Tweed. I've been an awful father and I don't expect her forgiveness. But I'd like to make amends and be there for her if and when she does need me."

For Lilly, this was the best response she could hope for. "I shouldn't judge you, but I will say that you have a wonderful daughter, Mr Pepper, and I do hope it's not too late for you to get to know her and see for yourself what you've missed."

He looked down, running the tip of his thumb around the rim of his cup. "I hope so as well. And you can call me James. There's no need for us to be so formal, is there?"

Lilly took a cloth and began to polish the counter. "James, it is then. And you can call me Lilly."

He smiled at her. "Thank you. If there's anything I can do, Lilly, please let me know. I imagine losing both an employee and a tenant will be difficult once Stacey transfers to London."

※

"**E**XCUSE ME?" LILLY said as her stomach clenched. James realised he'd said something he shouldn't have. "I apologise. It's just you asked why Stacey wasn't at school in London. I assumed you meant I should be using my position to help her get the best education possible. I was therefore going to talk to her about transferring in the Autumn. I'm sure she'd be glad to be studying in the city at one of the finest universities in the country."

Lilly threw the cloth under the counter and stiffened. "That's up to Stacey, don't you think?"

"Naturally. But I intend to give her the option I denied her before," he said reasonably.

Lilly nodded. "Yes, of course. What tea did Stacey brew for you?" she asked, eager to change the subject. Whatever decision Stacey made, she would support her, although it would be a dreadful loss if she left.

"A Chamomile. It's very nice."

"I think I'll have a cup."

Stacey returned from lunch just as she'd finished pouring. "How did your lunch with Bonnie go," she asked, joining Lilly behind the counter.

"It was interesting. I think Bonnie wants my help with the case."

A DEADLY SOLUTION

"Wow, really? Dad, Lilly's got quite famous round here since she solved a case in the Spring. People are always coming in asking how she did it."

"Yes, I read the article on-line. It was impressive. So, there's already a new case, is there? What is it this time?"

Lilly sighed. "It's a bit complicated. I was asked to attend a book club meeting recently to do a talk and demonstration of my teas. Unfortunately, at the end one of the women was found dead in the cloakroom. Murdered."

There was a sharp intake of breath from James.

"The police are having a difficult time identifying the weapon even with half of it still buried in her neck."

"That's interesting," James said. "They have half the murder weapon to hand, but still can't identify it? It must be something unusual."

Lilly nodded. "While Bonnie was in the bathroom, I took a picture of the case file," she added, pulling out her phone. "There was an x-ray of the victim's head and neck."

"Now that's better than being a cat burglar," Stacey teased. "Let me see, maybe we can help?"

Lilly showed Stacey the x-ray. "If you read the description, it's very odd. A Thin piece of metal with a pointed end. The other end snapped off so they don't know what the rest of it is or what it looked like. But it would have been longer."

Stacey looked puzzled. "I have no idea," she admitted. "Dad, what do you think?" she asked, spinning the phone round.

"Do you mind, Lilly?"

"No, go ahead."

James took the phone and peered intently at the image. "Mmm, I can't say for sure, but you know what this reminds me of?"

"What?" Lilly asked, suddenly alert.

"Have you ever heard of The Hatpin Panic?"

Stacey giggled. "No, but it sounds hilarious."

"Well, it was in a way. In other's not so much. He slid the phone back to Lilly. "I wrote a paper on it in my undergraduate years for an American Women's history course. It was an event that took place in the late eighteen to early nineteen hundreds. A woman named Leoti Blaker, a young Kansas woman visiting New York, was the victim of street harassment. Instead of putting up with the man attempting to take liberties with her, she elected instead to rip out her hatpin and stab him in the arm."

"Ha!" Stacey exclaimed. "Good for her."

"It started a movement," James continued enthusiastically, and Lilly could see the professor in him shining brightly. "More and more reports of women defending themselves from attacks using hatpins started cropping up with increasing frequency, all over the United States. In fact, one plucky woman in Chicago stopped a train robbery with her hatpin."

"That's incredible," Lilly said. "And very brave of her."

"Honestly, it was fascinating to study. The trend even spread here and to Australia. It was a fight for a woman's right to defend herself, but of course it became a hot topic political issue and was twisted into the safety of men. Should women be allowed to carry something so dangerous on their persons? After all, according to the politicians of the time, women were crazy and prone to hurt innocent people if given too much power."

"You're kidding me," Stacey said.

"I'm not," James said, shaking his head. "Things have changed now, thankfully, but it was very different back then. Men had never before experienced a time when women could and would defend themselves from attackers. They wanted to make hatpins illegal. There was a lot of debate and some laws were passed forbidding hatpins of certain lengths, but the whole movement was overshadowed with the break out of the war. Women's fashion shifted drastically after that, and they stopped using hatpins. The legal battle ended."

"I'm glad I didn't live in those times," Stacey said, with feeling. Lilly agreed with her.

"Sorry, that was a rather long-winded way of saying the picture reminded me of a hatpin."

"Don't apologise, dad, it was fascinating."

"Yes, but no doubt irrelevant. Women don't wear them anymore."

Lilly blinked. "Not usually, but..." she paused, thinking of Isadora and trying to recall if her hatpin was still in place after they'd found Jane. She couldn't remember.

"What is it, Lilly?" Stacey asked.

"One of the women at the book club was wearing a hat, and it was secured with a pin." She looked at the image again. "James, I think you just gave me my first lead."

"Yay!" Stacey cried. "Way to go, dad!"

Chapter Seven

AFTER THE SHOP had closed for the day, Lilly collected the teapot and tea blend Isadora Smith had ordered the day of the event. She'd long ago made it a habit to hand deliver, if possible, all orders for people living in Plumpton Mallet. It was a personal touch her customers appreciated, so it wasn't out of the ordinary for her to do it this time. Of course, her real motive was to make sure Isadora still had the hatpin she'd been wearing at the book club meeting.

Earl had already gone upstairs to the flat with Stacey, who'd volunteered to look after him while Lilly made her deliveries. Picking up the boxes, she went via the front door and unchained her bike. It was a beautiful evening, perfect for a leisurely bike ride.

As she rode she tried to think of a scenario whereby she could ask about the pin without it seeming obvious what she was up to. She also wondered what possible motive Isadora could have for the murder, but couldn't come up with anything. She didn't know Isadora or Jane at all, having met them both for the first time at Elizabeth's house, so being objective wouldn't be a problem. But at the same time, she didn't have any insider knowledge either. There had obviously been tension between Isadora and Elizabeth, Isadora herself had told her that. And then there was the spat at Lady Defoe's house, where Jane had been very rude to Elizabeth and made her look like a fool in front of everyone. Could Isadora have come to her friend's aid? Then there was Lady Gresham, the one to have found the body. But why would she have wanted to hurt Jane? Finally there was Abigail, who, at that moment, was the only one who appeared to have anything to gain from Jane Nolan's death. But it didn't seem to be the likeliest of motives.

It didn't take long to reach Isadora's home. It was a more modest abode than Elizabeth Davenport's, or the other women in the book club, apart from Abigail's, but it was still in the top tier of expensive homes in the area. She was just about to ring the bell on the gate, when the front door opened and Isadora waved. She must have seen her approach from the window and come to greet her.

"Lilly, what a lovely surprise," she said, unlocking and pulling open the iron gate. She was dressed more casually but still expensively in a floor-length skirt, silk blouse and with a designer scarf holding back her hair. "I wasn't expecting you so soon. Did my teapot arrive?"

"It did," Lilly replied, pushing her bike down the short drive towards the door. "I thought I'd deliver it to you myself."

"Oh, how lovely of you, I do so appreciate the personal touch. It's so rare nowadays. If you're not busy, would you like to come in for a cup of tea? I can christen my new pot."

Lilly smiled, she had been banking on Isadora's sense of hospitality. She was certainly the friendliest of all the women in the book club. "I'd love to, thank you." It would give her a chance to try to work the hatpin into the conversation.

She leaned her bike against a small tree and followed Isadora through to a large kitchen where she gave her the boxes. Isadora tore into the one containing the teapot like a child on Christmas morning. She held it up to admire before rinsing it out and opening the tea.

"I just love this Chamomile. I've been craving a cup since the book club."

While Isadora made the tea, Lilly asked how she'd been since the death of her friend.

"As well as can be expected in the circumstances, I suppose. I spoke with her boyfriend yesterday, he's absolutely distraught. He told me he'd been planning to ask Jane to be his wife."

Lilly frowned. "Oh, how awful, I didn't realise she was in a serious relationship. Is it anyone I would know?"

"It's Lady Gresham's brother, Theodore. Lord Gresham. Yes, they were besotted apparently."

"Oh," Lilly said, making a mental note. She hadn't realised Lady Gresham had been so close to Jane that she was about to become her sister-in-law. It seemed the members of the book club were more intimate than she'd initially thought. "Poor man, no wonder Lady Gresham was so distraught if

Jane was to become part of the family. I realise now it was a double shock to find her as she did."

"Yes, it is terribly upsetting to all of us who knew her," Isadora said, wringing her hands. "Jane really was such a lovely person."

This was definitely a different tune to the one she'd been singing during their private chat at Elizabeth's house. The way she'd talked about Jane's incident at Lady Defoe's house at Easter hadn't shown Jane in a good light at all. But perhaps it was simply a case of remembering only the good things and conveniently forgetting the bad when someone had died. Or not wishing to speak ill of the dead. Nonetheless, Lilly got the impression Isadora had some conflicting feelings towards Jane.

"Were you and Jane on good terms? I don't mean to be rude, I just got the sense there was some tension the other day."

Isadora laughed. "Dear Lilly, there's always some tension in our circles; it's just the way it is. We were on excellent terms. If anything, I've been locking horns with Elizabeth more these days. While I hate to condone Jane's crude behaviour at Easter, she did have a point when she called Elizabeth out that day. But that's how it goes in friendships, isn't it? We snip and snipe at each other occasionally, then a few days later we're at the book club, or luncheon, or a dinner dance and everything is as right as rain again."

Lilly wasn't sure she agreed. It wasn't anything like the friendships she had, it sounded exhausting truth be told. But she didn't argue. The kettle began to whistle and Isadora brewed the tea the same way Lilly had shown them all, then poured them both a cup. "Oh, heavenly," she said.

"I'm glad you've found a tea to enjoy."

"Oh, I adore many teas. I usually order them from a shop in London, but I will certainly be purchasing what I need from your Tea Emporium from now on," she said. "You really do know your stuff."

"Thank you. And talking of shopping," Lilly said, hoping she was making a smooth transition and not sounding bonkers, or worse, suspicious. "That hatpin you were wearing the other day? Would you mind if I had another look at it? I thought it was just stunning and would like to show it to the local antique shop owner in town and ask her to be on the lookout for something similar for me."

"You wear hats with hatpins?" Isadora asked. "How lovely, there's not many of us left, you know. Yes, I'll just go and get it."

Lilly kept smiling until Isadora had left the room then sighed deeply. If she still had her pin and in one piece then it obviously wasn't the murder weapon. A moment later she arrived back with the butterfly pin, along with another, its match. "I love these," she said. "I tend to collect sets, but these really are my favourites."

Lilly took a picture with her phone. "They are very pretty, so intricate. I hope I can find something as nice for myself."

They finished their tea and Isadora walked Lilly to the door. "Thank you again for delivering my order, and so promptly."

"You're very welcome. Thank you for your hospitality," Lilly replied. They said goodbye and Isadora went back inside, saying she'd see to the gate later.

Lilly was a bit disappointed. But looking at the hatpins again, she felt sure it was more than similar to the item Jane Nolan had been stabbed with. Perhaps it wasn't so far-fetched after all to believe a hatpin was the murder weapon, even if it wasn't Isadora's. *I think I'll talk to Bonnie and see what she thinks...*

Lilly walked over to her bike deep in thought when a car came speeding up the drive, clipping her bike wheel and knocking it over. "No!" Lilly exclaimed in surprise, just as Abigail Douglas got out of the car screeching about what a stupid place to park a bike.

"My car," she wailed, but Lilly could tell this time it was an act.

"My bike," she countered, glaring at Abigail.

Abigail walked to the front of her car to examine the bumper. "You're lucky that bike didn't damage my car."

"You're the one who hit my bike. It better not be damaged, Abigail." Lilly snapped.

They glared at each other for a moment, then realised where they both were.

"What are you doing here?" they both said at the same time.

"**A**CTUALLY, ON SECOND thoughts Abigail, there's no need to tell me. I know exactly why you're here, to interview Isadora."

"Of course I am. I'm writing the story on the case."

"And I suppose Archie knows what you're up to?"

"First of all, what happens at the paper is no concern of yours. Secondly, he is well aware I am covering this story. I was there when Jane was killed. I have insider, first-hand knowledge and the powers that be have agreed I should be the one to take the lead on this. So you don't need to worry about your little friend. I'm interviewing all the ladies who were present. Not you though, Lilly. I mean all the *important* ladies."

Lilly picked up her bike, checked there was no damage and mounted, ready to leave. "Well, good luck, Abigail."

"You didn't tell me why *you* were here," she said, stepping in front of the bike and blocking her path. "You're not looking into this case, too, are you? I've told you to leave it to those of us who are qualified."

"Oh, grow up, Abigail. If you must know I was delivering Isadora's order, it arrived today. I always personally deliver orders to customers in Plumpton Mallet. Now, if you'll get out of my way, I'd like to leave..."

As she manoeuvred the bike around Abigail and passed the side of her car, she caught a glimpse of the side light and couldn't help but laugh.

"What? What is it?" demanded Abigail, stalking to the side of her vehicle. "My car! You've ruined my car."

"It was patently obvious, even to a blind man riding a fast horse, that you hit my bike on purpose, so you have no one to blame but yourself. Goodbye, Abigail," she said, and she sped off up the drive, eager to be away.

As she cycled back to town, she spotted the local antique shop, still doing a brisk trade with tourists. *They must open later in the summer, lucky for me.* She parked her bike at the front and peered through at the window display to see if she could spot any hatpins for sale. There weren't any, so she went inside.

"Hello, welcome to Rosie's Antiques," the elderly lady behind the counter said.

"Hello, I was wondering if you sold hatpins?"

"I do indeed," she said, leading Lilly toward the back of the shop where a number of antique pins were on display, sitting on red velvet inside a locked display case. "As you can see, I have quite a few. Most of them dated just prior to the turn of the twentieth century."

Lilly leaned forward and looked more closely. They were beautiful and obviously old, but more to the point they were very similar to the metal on the x-ray. Lilly felt a surge of hope that she'd found the identity of the murder weapon. She walked back towards the counter where the owner had returned.

"You have a lovely selection. Do you get a lot of people in here looking for hatpins?"

"Oh, yes, they don't stay on the shelves very long. It's amazing how popular they are considering they aren't used much nowadays. There are quite a number of collectors around Plumpton Mallet, actually."

Hearing this, Lilly made her excuses and went back outside to call Bonnie.

"Lilly? What can I do for you?"

"Bonnie, I'm at Rosie's antiques in town, do you know it?"

"Yes, why?"

"Well, I'm feeling reasonably confident that the murder weapon used to kill Jane Nolan was an antique hatpin.

I've already spoken to Isadora Smith, I had to go anyway to deliver her teapot, and the one she was wearing that day she still has. But I'm thinking any one of those women could own them. According to the shop keeper here there are a lot of collectors around town."

"That's very interesting, well done, Lilly. I spoke to the pathologist earlier, and he was still at a loss, he was swaying toward the idea of it being a broach, but apart from his feeling that it would be too difficult to wield in the way needed in order to pierce the victim's throat, he also felt the back pin wouldn't have been long enough. I'll throw the hatpin theory his way and see if he can confirm. In the meantime, I'll do a follow up at Rosie's Antique shop and see if she has a list of local customers that have bought these pins. I'll check with other shops in the area too. It's all a bit of a long shot as the murder weapon could have been a family heirloom, or bought abroad or something, but it needs following up."

"Good idea," Lilly said. "I'll go back inside and take some pictures of the ones here. I'll send them to you to pass on to the pathologist."

"I appreciate that, thanks Lilly."

"Okay, speak soon." Lilly hung up and returned to the display case inside the shop. "Do you mind if I take a few pictures of these?" she asked, holding up her phone.

"Not at all."

Lilly took several images of the whole array of pins and forwarded them on to Bonnie, then something in another case caught her attention. "Oh, this is nice." It looked to be French porcelain although there was no marking and had a hand painted cherry blossom design finished with a gold rim. It was an unusual triangular cup with triple foot and a matching saucer. Definitely a cabinet piece and would look fabulous in the shop. She decided to buy it and put it on the counter just as her phone rang. It was Stacey.

"Hi, is everything all right."

"Yeah, fine. Just wanted to let you know that Lady Defoe's tea set has arrived."

"Are you in the shop?"

"No, Earl and me were upstairs when I heard knocking. I went downstairs and signed for it."

"Perfect, Stacey, thank you. I might come back and pick them up. Do you think Lady Defoe would mind me delivering this evening?"

"No, I don't think so, she'll be glad to have them, I'll bet. Besides, she's too polite to refuse you and if she's not there, you can always go again another day."

"Yes, you're right, Stacey, but it's..." she looked at her watch, "Nearly half-past six. Could you do me a favour and ring her to see if it's all right? Her number is on the order form in the storeroom. Text me back and let me know, would you?"

"Sure, no problem, give me a couple of minutes."

Lilly hung up and turned back to the shop owner. "Sorry about that. I'd like to take this cup and saucer, please."

"It's lovely, isn't it? No maker's mark, hence the price, but it's an unusual and very pretty little piece." As she wrapped it up, she looked at Lilly with a smile. "You know Lady Defoe?"

"Sort of. She ordered a tea set from my shop recently."

"She's a lovely woman. She was in here just this morning as a matter of fact with her husband and Lord Gresham and his sister, Lady Gresham. Well, there you are, my dear. Enjoy it."

Lilly took the well wrapped china from her, paid and left the shop with a promise to return when time allowed. Just as she put the parcel in the bike's basket, a text from Stacey came through to confirm Lady Defoe would be very pleased for Lilly to deliver her tea set. She mounted her bike and returned to the shop.

*T*HE TEA SET Lady Defoe had ordered was too large to fit in the bicycle basket, so Lilly picked up her car from home and drove to the Defoe house. Although on the same side of the river as the homes of the other ladies, it was by far the largest. With the drive being twice the length and the well maintained and well established gardens, set over several acres, it looked like a painting. Once again Lilly was reminded of a setting for a novel, this time Ferndean Manor from Charlotte Bronte's Jane Eyre, although it wasn't quite as large. It had apparently been in the family for at least five generations, with each generation adding to the house to make it bigger and grander.

There was a turning circle set outside the house with a central fountain surrounded by box hedge. Lilly parked and was retrieving the order from the boot of her car when she heard the sound of footsteps coming down the flight of stone steps. It was obviously the housekeeper.

"Good evening, Miss Tweed, let me help you with those boxes. Lady Defoe is expecting you, if you'd like to follow me."

"Thank you."

She was taken through the large foyer with its enormous central chandelier, marble floor and stained glass windows, along a panelled hallway and through to the rear of the house. Lady Defoe and her guests were gathered in a large sun room which overlooked swathes of manicured lawn, woodland, the river and finally the edge of the town itself before taking in the sweeping moorland at the opposite side of the valley.

Lady Defoe and Lady Gresham were seated on a large cushioned sofa talking, while two men she assumed were Lady Defoe's husband and Lady Gresham's brother Theodore were sitting at a green baize card table, playing what looked to Lilly's eagle eye, poker.

"Miss Lillian Tweed, Ma'am," the housekeeper announced, depositing the boxes she had carried on a nearby table, then departed.

"Lilly, welcome," Lady Defoe said, rising gracefully from her seat and coming to greet her. "Come and have a seat. I believe you know, Lady Gresham? And this is her brother, Theodore and my husband."

Lilly said hello to the two men, then took a seat opposite the ladies, handing the largest box to Lady Defoe. She carefully opened it and withdrew the teapot first, holding it up to the light to admire it, just as Isadora had done with hers. "It's simply beautiful, isn't it?" she asked the room at large.

"Very beautiful," Lady Gresham agreed. "It's the same set Elizabeth ordered the other day, if I'm not mistaken. You must have similar tastes."

Lady Defoe raised an eyebrow. "Yes, I'm sure that's what it is, Meredith. Now Lilly, will you stay and have tea with us? It would be lovely to have you share my set's inaugural outing."

"I'd love to. Thank you," she replied, hoping she wouldn't be expected to serve.

Lady Defoe rang a bell and at the housekeeper's return gave her explicit instructions, then turned to the men. "Gentleman, we're having tea on the patio shortly. We'll meet you there."

Lord Defoe smiled fondly at his wife's joy in her newest acquisition. "Lovely," he said. "I could do with some tea. Theo's wiping me out and I'm afraid I'm about to lose the family silver."

The ladies made their way outside to a comfortable seating area under an awning where the warmth of the evening sun and the fragrance of the surrounding roses made Lilly feel as though she were on holiday somewhere exotic. Moments later the housekeeper returned with the tray and the gentlemen joined them shortly after.

"Shall I do the honours?" Lady Gresham asked, lifting the pot and filling their cups.

"Do you know," Lady Gresham said to the men. "Lilly has an amazing knowledge of teas. She's quite the expert. The talk and demonstration she gave at the book club was fascinating. I never knew there were so many health benefits and remedies."

Theodore Gresham shifted uncomfortably in his seat, catching Lilly's eye briefly then glancing away.

"Are you all right, Theo?" Lady Defoe asked.

"It's nothing," he said, fixing a smile in place, but only a few minutes into their tea he excused himself and went indoors.

"Oh dear, Meredith, perhaps you should go and check on your brother? He's obviously not well."

Lady Gresham sighed. "It's Jane. I should have known better than to bring up the book club in front of him. Excuse me." She rose and followed her brother inside.

Lord Defoe shook his head. "Your friend has a nasty habit of upsetting her brother, my dear." He said to his wife.

Lilly sat sipping her tea and keeping quiet, watching and listening as the drama played out. Perhaps she'd learn something interesting.

"It's not her fault. Theo is hurting terribly, which is only to be expected. But I'm sure she didn't mean any harm."

"He's in an awful state, poor man," said Lord Defoe. "He was in love and was going to ask the girl to marry him from what he's been telling me."

Lady Defoe nodded. "Yes, that's what Meredith thinks, too. Of course, she wasn't very happy about it."

"Now don't start gossiping, my dear," Lord Defoe said, with a quick glance at Lilly.

"Oh, Lilly was there, darling, and took control while the others were too shocked to do anything remotely helpful from what I heard. She's one of us now. Isn't that right, Lilly?"

Lilly nodded. "It was a dreadful thing to have happened. I didn't realise Lord Gresham was so close to Jane. He must be heartbroken, especially if his sister didn't approve. That must have made things much more difficult?"

"You're right on every count, Lilly. Meredith was not very happy at Theo's interest in Jane. She always had something negative to say whenever they'd spent time together. You see, Meredith never thought Jane was good enough for Theo. She came from new money, with no status as it were, and unfortunately she just couldn't look past it."

Lord Defoe scoffed. "Honestly! Who really cares about that nonsense nowadays? It's ludicrous. Poor Theo feels as though he can't talk to his sister about this tragedy because he knows how she really felt about Jane. He's feeling very alone at the moment. I've told him he can come here and drink my scotch and get it off his chest whenever he wants."

"That's good of you, dear. I feel as you do about the whole thing. It's hard enough to find love these days as it is. I do feel it very hypocritical of Meredith. If Jane was good enough for her to befriend, then why not her brother? I mean, look at the members of the book club. None of them apart from Meredith are titled, yet she spends all her time with them."

"Exactly," Lord Defoe said. "If they're good enough for Meredith, then they ought to be good enough for her brother."

Lilly lifted the tea pot and refilled their cups, wondering if Meredith Gresham's motive for surrounding herself with the untitled was because she would therefore always be the queen bee among them.

"Thank you, Lilly. You know, out of all those women who made up Elizabeth Davenport's circle, I always liked Jane the best."

"Why is that?" Lilly asked, taking a biscuit the housekeeper had brought with the tea tray.

"Jane Nolan was a woman who knew who and what she was, and what she wanted from life. There were no airs and graces, what you saw is what you got, a terrible cliché but perfectly true. When Theodore first showed interest, she turned him away. Remarkable, isn't it? Now if the shoe was on the other foot, any one of those other women would have snapped his hand off and dragged him down the aisle before he knew what was happening simply because of his title, but not Jane. She didn't have a sycophantic bone in her body. She honestly didn't care about any of that. She wanted to take her time, let the relationship grow naturally to make sure they were compatible before committing. Do you know he tried the ultimate grand gesture once, offering to fly her to Paris for dinner? She turned him down and said she rather go to the movies. In my book, that was the mark of a woman comfortable in her own skin but genuine at the same time."

"I think that's partly the reason he was so fascinated by her," Lord Gresham added perceptively. "She made him work a bit harder than any of the others."

"Yes, I believe you're right there."

They continued with tea and the subject changed to less serious matters. When some time had gone by, and it was apparent that the Gresham's would not be returning, Lilly made her excuses.

"Thank you for your hospitality, it's been lovely."

"You're very welcome, Lilly, and thank you for coming all this way yourself to deliver my wonderful china. No doubt I will see you again soon. I have every intention of purchasing my tea from you in the future."

85

Lilly said goodbye to them both and assured them she could find her own way out. In the hall, she found Meredith Gresham returning.

"Oh, are you leaving?"

"Yes, I have to get back."

"That's a shame. I apologise for the interruption. It was rude of us to disappear like that, but I'm afraid I inadvertently upset my brother and had to check on him. He's a little better now, but isn't up to coming back for tea."

"I understand." Lilly said, and Meredith smiled and went on her way to rejoin her hosts.

As Lilly ascended the steps, she spotted Theodore Gresham at the fountain, fiddling with a small cigar and a lighter. Seeing Lilly, he stuffed them in his pocket. "Leaving so soon?" he asked.

"Yes, I'm afraid I have things to be getting on with." She paused for a moment. "I hope you don't think I'm speaking out of turn, but I've just come to understand how close you and Jane actually were. I'd like to say how very sorry I am for your loss."

Theodore blushed. "Kind of you. Thanks."

"I hope you have someone to turn to, to talk things through with? It helps to have that kind of support."

"Yes. Actually, Jane's friend Isadora has been very kind. We've spoken a few times since it happened, which has helped."

"I'm sure it would help your sister to be able to talk things through too. She's obviously upset for you, but I suspect because she's been critical of your relationship in the past, she now feels as though she can't help you because her intentions might not be welcomed as genuine. She doesn't want to overstep, I think. But she does care."

"You're very astute."

Lilly nodded and smiled. "I was the agony aunt at the paper for years. I've seen my fair share of heartache and loss."

Lord Gresham nodded. "That explains it. Well, I better be getting back."

Lilly watched him stride towards the house wondering at the odd relationship Jane Nolan had had with the Gresham's; loved by one sibling, loathed by the other. Could it have had something to do with her murder?

Chapter Eight

*T*HE NEXT DAY was Stacey's day off, so Lilly and Earl were alone in the shop. It seemed a long time since it had just been the two of them and she had to admit she was looking forward to it. Stacey was a godsend to her business, but the recent immersion in the world of the rich and aristocratic of Plumpton Mallet had left her feeling grubby, and she wanted time alone to process it all.

As she set the shop up and brewed herself a pot of mint tea, she thought about what she'd learned since Jane Nolan's death. Apart from Jane, who hadn't been friendly when they met, and in hindsight that could have been her response to Elizabeth as opposed to her, and Abigail who wasn't worth mentioning, she had, on the surface at least, been made to feel very welcome by all the woman. On the face of it they were all good friends, but now she knew there was an underlying current of cattiness and one-upmanship between all of them, it muddied the waters in terms of finding a motive and the person responsible for killing Jane.

Meredith, while proclaiming friendship to her face, didn't like Jane due to her relationship with her brother Theo. Would she have gone so far as to get rid of Jane to prevent the marriage? Elizabeth had been acutely embarrassed at Easter by Jane's acerbic tongue. Perhaps it wasn't the first time she'd been on the receiving end of such an insult and had decided enough was enough? Isadora, while agreeing with Jane's comments, admitted she came to the defence of her friend Elizabeth, but then said she and Jane had also butted heads. What about? And would it be enough of a motive for her to get rid of Jane? If she was right and a hatpin was used as a murder weapon then Isadora was probably out of the equation because she still had hers. But if it wasn't hers then where did it come from?

Lady Defoe, while not a suspect due to her not attending the book club meeting, admitted she liked Jane the most due to her non sycophantic behaviour. But she intimated her thoughts ran to believing the rest of them were little more than social climbers. Did anyone in this group genuinely like the others? It seemed not.

And then there was Abigail. How she had managed to become part of this social circle, Lilly didn't know. Possibly with promises of favourable articles in the paper, an uncharitable thought perhaps, but she wouldn't put it past her. Abigail was definitely the one person in that group who had ideas above her station. The epitome of the social climber the others had been accused of. But would she have committed murder in order to prove herself and keep her job? A job that she had admitted was her last chance. Somehow Lilly couldn't see it, but at this stage she had to keep an open mind. So far every single one of the woman was a suspect with a motive. How on earth could she narrow it down?

*I*T APPEARED EARL was in an unusually social mood that day as he jumped onto the counter and lay down near the till. The customers found it adorable, and he received many strokes and ear scratches, as well as quite a few cuddles as the day went by. Several people had insisted on taking photographs with him, so no doubt he would also be all over the Internet before the day was out. She made a note for Stacey so she could add them to The Tea Emporium's social media sites. Perhaps her former stray would become a viral sensation?

It was mid afternoon and Lilly was just contemplating shutting the shop for five minutes while she went out to grab a sandwich, when the bell above the door rang and James Pepper walked in. Lilly wondered when he had time to teach, considering he was in her shop so often. Or maybe he'd taken some of his owed holiday?

"Hello, James."

"Good afternoon, Lilly. Is Stacey about?"

"No, it's her day off today."

"Is she upstairs, do you know?"

"I think she's out actually."

James looked a little annoyed at this. *Surely if he wanted to see his daughter he would be better making a specific arrangement rather than just turning up and expecting her to be here?* Lilly thought.

"Have you tried phoning her?"

"Of course. There was no answer. Honestly!"

Lilly sighed, which was a mistake as James Pepper immediately took it as a criticism.

"Do you have something to say, Lilly?"

"No, James, I have nothing to say."

Good grief, this man was unbelievable. One minute he was nice and calm, friendly and helpful, the next irritated and on the verge of exploding. It reminded her of Abigail.

"It looks as though you do. Go on, what is it? I'm interested in what you have to say."

James Pepper was obviously looking for a fight. She took a deep breath, willing herself to stay calm.

"Honestly? I don't think you should expect Stacey to be constantly at your beck and call. She's an adult with a life of her own."

"She's my daughter."

"I'm not disputing that, but she has her own life to lead, too."

"But I am her father," he said, raising his voice.

"I know," Lilly said, raising hers in response and causing Earl to sit up, ears twitching.

"Then please stop interfering in the relationship between me and my daughter. It's nothing to do with you."

"Fine," Lilly said, raising both hands. She did not want this to escalate; James Pepper was obviously in a foul mood for some reason.

"Now, let's start again. Do you know where Stacey is?"

"No, I don't. She doesn't take many days off, so I imagine she had plans. If she turns up then I'll let her know you're looking for her. Now, I think you'd better leave. With Stacey absent there's no reason for you to stay."

He snorted but did not raise his voice this time. "I know you feel threatened by me."

"I'm sorry?"

"You know Stacey will be leaving and coming to London soon," he said. "And you're naturally worried about losing both an employee and a tenant. But there's no need to be so aggressive whenever I turn up."

Lilly was stunned for a moment and just stared at him. "Me? Me, aggressive? You come into my shop and start shouting at... you know what? Never mind, James. I have no intention of arguing with you."

James tutted, shook his head and left.

Lilly picked up Earl, giving him soothing strokes. "Don't worry, Earl, he's gone, thank goodness. And I have no idea what that was all about."

It was almost closing time before Lilly had a spare moment to herself. The height of summer had brought tourists and locals out in force, and nearly all of them had walked into her shop. She was just finding her keys to lock the door when it opened.

"Good evening, Lilly. I've got that paint you ordered."

"Oh, Jim! I'm so glad you caught me before I closed because I had completely forgotten you were coming with it today."

She had ordered some specialist paint as the shop sign needed a touch up and she had intended to do it before she went home.

"Didn't you need it today?" he asked to confirm.

"Yes, I did. Thanks so much for dropping it in, I really appreciate it."

"Are you about to close?" he asked, putting the paint cans inside the door.

"I was. Why, did you need something?"

"The kids had an accident and broke the teapot. I thought maybe you could have fixed it, but my wife said she'd like a new one. I told her I'd come and have a look at what you've got when I brought the paint. Do you mind? If you're going to be here for a while painting, anyway?"

"Not at all," Lilly said. "Let me pay you for the paint and you can have a look round while I'm working outside. I'll put the closed sign up so no one else comes in while I'm trying to paint." She went to the till and paid with cash, taking the paid invoice from Jim, then went to the storeroom for ladders.

On the way back through the shop, she found Jim playing with Earl rather than looking at tea pots and laughed. "Caught you," she said on the way out the door. Jim laughed. "Well, he's a very nice cat."

With paint and brushes in hand, she climbed the ladder while Jim browsed. It was a very good job he was in the shop as she would be in need of a witness very soon; Abigail Douglas had just pulled up outside and as was her wont she did not look pleased.

*L*ILLY'S ENTIRE BODY tensed at the sight of Abigail Douglas. She truly was fed up to the back teeth of her constant appearance and petulance. She seemed to take great joy in getting Lilly's back up and deliberately goading her. It was bad enough meeting her on terra firma, but at the top of a ladder, paint can and brush in hand, it was more than a little nerve-wracking, because you just never knew what she would do. She slammed her car door and stomped over to Lilly, seething with so much rage she was practically vibrating.

"Good evening, Abigail," Lilly said, trying to be sincere but failing miserably. Between Abigail Douglas and James Pepper, her patience was wearing so thin as to be almost transparent. It felt as though every time she met Abigail she ended up on the receiving end of an unwarranted tirade. Her natural response to the woman now was to tense up and become defensive and she didn't like the feeling. She'd never felt this way before meeting Abigail, and wondered if her shortness with James earlier was due to having to be constantly on guard and defending herself.

"Don't you *good evening, Abigail* me! You're at it again, Lillian Tweed."

She remained at the top of the ladder, her back to Abigail, while she continued working on the sign. She'd rested the paint can on the narrow top step of the ladder where she could dip in her brush easily. *If I hurry up and finish, I can leave. It's not likely she'll follow me home to harass me.*

"What am I supposed to have done this time?" she asked, without looking down. She didn't want Abigail to realise she was actually beginning to get to her.

"You had tea at Lady Defoe's house, and with the Gresham's there!" Abigail circled the bottom of the ladder, trying to catch Lilly's eye.

Lilly snorted, swallowing the mirth that had begun to bubble up. She couldn't help finding it amusing. "That's what you're concerned about? The fact I had tea with our titled locals? I can't believe how shallow you are, Abigail. Or are you moving into gossip columns now?"

"How dare you? I am not a gossip columnist." She exclaimed. But Lilly knew from Archie that Abigail had pitched that very idea to the senior executives at the gazette not long after she'd arrived. The idea had been shot down. They wanted to remain a professional paper, not a rag whose primary type of journalism was to report on whom had been seen with whom among the most notable of the Plumpton Mallet residents.

"So, what exactly is your problem now?"

"You know very well what it is. You are constantly stepping on my toes and trying to play detective. Well, I am not going to put up with it any more. This is my story. You are a menace, Lillian Tweed."

Lilly finally snapped, all vestiges of the previous mirth vanishing in an instant. "Right! That's it, Abigail Douglas. I refuse to be the punching bag for your ludicrous insecurities any more. You need to take a long hard look at yourself and ask why people no longer write to you? Stop harassing me or I will get an injunction taken out against you. You are borderline insane, Abigail. Get a grip on yourself before you do or say something that will get you into serious trouble. Trouble you may not get out of."

Lilly was surprised at herself, she'd never lost her temper like this before, but she'd absolutely reached her limit. Abigail hadn't expected it either, and true to form reacted badly to what she perceived as insults rather than the home truths they actually were. She approached the ladder and gave it a swift, hard kick.

"Ah!" Lilly wailed as the ladder wobbled dangerously. She grabbed the sign to prevent it falling completely, but the paint can was now balanced precariously with no support. It fell, hitting Abigail on the shoulder and splattering thick black oil paint all over her clothes, one side of her face and her hair, before bouncing to the ground where it covered her shoes.

Abigail stared at the mess in absolute horror. Then gave Lilly the blackest look she ever had. *Literally*, Lilly thought as she watched the ink coloured paint drip off Abigail's chin.

"You'll pay for that, Lillian Tweed," she hissed through clenched teeth. "Do you hear me? I'm calling the police and you are going to pay for assaulting me!"

Lilly was about to give Abigail a piece of her mind for even suggesting this was her fault, when Jim exited the shop. "I saw that, Ms Douglas. What did you think you were doing? You're lucky Lilly didn't fall off the ladder and break her neck! This was all your doing and if you dare suggest otherwise, *I* will be the one calling the police.

Abigail clearly had not expected there to be a witness to her abhorrent behaviour and started stuttering.

Lilly climbed down the ladder on shaking legs, looked at Abigail and shook her head. *What a mess.* She turned to Jim, "Thanks, Jim, I appreciate your support. Abigail," she said.

"Jim is right, what you did was dangerous and could have resulted in me having a serious accident, or worse. I refuse to deal with your tantrums anymore, and if you do anything remotely like this again, I'll see to that you are prosecuted. Do you understand me?"

Abigail nodded; seemingly mute as it suddenly dawned on her how serious the situation was.

"Now, if you walk round to the back of the shop, I'll let you in through the storeroom to use the bathroom and get cleaned up as much as you can."

"I'll go with her," Jim said, still frowning. "I suggest you thank Lilly, Ms Douglas. She is being far more magnanimous than I'd be in the same circumstances."

"Thank you," she said in a small voice.

Lilly nodded curtly. "Did you find a teapot, Jim?"

"Yes, I put it on the counter."

"All right, I'll deal with that while you're escorting Abigail."

Lilly went back inside with the ladder, a now empty paint can and the brushes, putting them in the storeroom before opening the back door. Back in the shop, she rang up Jim's sale and wrapped it. A moment later, with Abigail using the bathroom, Jim reappeared with her bag, which he'd carried for her to prevent it getting covered in paint. He put it on the counter.

"I'll bring some sand round shortly to cover the paint on the pavement. It should soak most of it up and make it easier to clean. I'll pressure wash it for you first thing."

"Thanks, Jim, you're a life saver."

"Are you all right, Lilly?"

97

"Yes, I think so. Still shocked that Abigail would go so far. We have an interesting history, to say the least. Perhaps I shouldn't have snapped at her."

"Don't feel guilty about snapping at her, Lilly. From where I was standing, she deserved it and more. It's not normal behaviour you know. I honestly think that woman needs professional help. Do you need me to stay until she leaves?"

Lilly shook her head. "No, I'm fine, Jim, but thank you. Abigail has completely embarrassed and shocked herself, and I think she'll calm down in order to save face. How long she remains in the bathroom is another thing. But I've got a good book with me so I'll be fine."

"All right, well, I'll start the clean up outside. Thanks again for the teapot. Look after yourself, Lilly, and remember I'm not far away if you need me."

WHILE ABIGAIL WAS in the bathroom, Lilly decided to call Archie. If anyone knew the true story about Abigail being put on the murder inquiry legitimately it would be him.

She stood behind the counter, one hand on the phone pressed to her ear, the other scratching an ecstatic cat who was purring very loudly.

"Archie Brown," said a harried voice at the other end of the line.

"Archie, it's Lilly," she said, keeping an eye on the back of the shop in case Abigail appeared. "Have you got a minute to talk?"

"Hi, Lilly. Yes, what is it?"

"Nothing new, just being harassed by Abigail Douglas for a change," she said, and Archie grunted. "Listen, she's been telling me she's been put in charge of the Jane Nolan story and I wanted to double check with you to see if that's right? I've come to the point where I don't believe a thing that comes out of her mouth."

"I wouldn't either, the woman's a pathological liar," Archie said. "She's not been put in charge of that story at all, and I'll tell you why that would be inappropriate; because she's a prime suspect. Personally, I don't believe she did it, but the police are interested in her for obvious reasons."

"Really?"

"Of course. I spoke with Bonnie earlier and it looks as though they haven't managed to narrow it down much at all. She's under a lot of pressure from the higher ups to get this sorted out quickly. You really are the only person out of all the attendees they have crossed off their list, because you didn't have any opportunity to kill Jane. Everyone else was inside alone at one point or another while Jane was in the cloakroom. Any one of them could have walked in on her, quickly stabbed her and returned to the party without being detected."

"Including Abigail," Lilly said. Silently thanking Elizabeth Davenport for informing the police that she had been outside or in the garden room the entire time, therefore keeping her off the suspect list.

"Exactly. It's a conflict of interest at the very least, so we would never have even contemplated putting her on the story. This is just another incident of Abigail trying to secure her currently precarious position at the paper," Archie explained. "She's continually trying to make a splash. She was hired as an agony aunt but has completely ruined it. The column is a disaster, as is her advice. Nobody is writing to her, Lilly. Her job security really isn't looking good. I don't think she had this kind of problem where she was before, even though it's the same owners, but of course they didn't have you to compare her to. And her previous paper wrote a different type of news if you get my drift. People appreciated and believed in your advice, Lilly, they still do, which of course is part of the problem. But it's not yours."

"Thanks, Archie, I appreciate you saying so," Lilly said, double checking Abigail wasn't listening to the conversation. "So, Abigail, really is a suspect?"

"According to Bonnie she is, and even if I don't agree, I understand why. There's no proof she isn't for one thing. In fact there's barely any proof at all to say who committed the crime. Everyone knows Abigail is desperate for a story and a little unhinged..."

"I'll say," Lilly replied with feeling, the near miss on the ladder fresh in her mind.

"Yes, but it means there's potential there for her having *created* the story, if you know what I mean? It might be far-fetched, but it's no weaker a motive than the ones they're thinking about for the others. It's one of the reasons Bonnie is having such a difficult time with this case. They can't pin down a motive."

Lilly felt a fluttering in her chest. The same thought had occurred to her, but could Abigail really have killed Jane just to get a story? She'd just tried to kick a ladder out from underneath her so she obviously had some pent up rage, but surely that would be one step too far? "Thanks for the information, Archie," Lilly said, suddenly remembering Abigail's handbag was on the counter. "I'll let you go. Talk to you soon."

"You will do. Bye, Lilly."

Lilly hung up and checked the storeroom door. Abigail was obviously still in the bathroom, so she pulled the bag closer and opened it. Immediately she found a large spiral notebook, she took it out and began to read.

She had a number of notes on Jane's murder, specifically those involving Elizabeth Davenport. *If Abigail is compiling legitimate evidence on the case, then it seems unlikely that's she's the guilty party,* Lilly thought.

"What do you think you're doing?" Abigail shouted. "What gives you the right to go through my bag?" She marched across the room, hair a glutinous mess and a dirty shade of grey dripping with oily water and reeking of turpentine. She snatched the notebook from Lilly's hand before she'd had a chance to read any of the notes.

"What gives you the right to try to cause me serious injury by knocking me off a ladder?" Lilly countered. This drastically changed Abigail's tune.

"Fine," she said. Sighing and taking a seat at the counter and putting her head in her hands. She'd done her best with turpentine and soap and water, but the stains of black paint were still unmissable. She looked an absolute fright.

"Do you want a cup of tea?" Lilly said, beginning to feel a little sorry for her. Abigail nodded. "Then, perhaps we can call a truce and share what we know? To be frank, I'm sick of fighting with you. It's exhausting and dispiriting and I have better things to do with my time. Are you agreeable? Because if not, you can leave now."

Abigail nodded again.

"Right, then in the spirit of our new found détente, I need to tell you you're being thought of as a suspect by the police, Abigail." She said, spooning leaves into a pot and switching on the kettle.

Abigail looked up. "What?"

"I was looking to see if I could find anything incriminating."

"I'm a... what are you talking about? Why would I be a suspect? Who told you that?"

"Apparently the police have no reason to rule you out. You were there on the day..."

"So were you."

"But I never went into the main house apart from when I first arrived, and that was before anyone else had turned up. The next time was at the end when Meredith screamed. The furthest I went during the day was the garden room, other than right at the beginning when I went to the kitchen to fill the kettles. All of you, including Jane, were in the pergola then. So you see it couldn't possibly have been me. Now, since you had time to be alone with Jane, the police can't rule you out as a suspect. You had the opportunity and the police feel you also have a motive. While the other women also had the opportunity, the police are struggling to find a decent reason for any of them to kill Jane."

"I don't have a motive. But I have evidence."

"None that I saw," Lilly countered, pouring them both a tea and sliding Abigail's cup and saucer to her across the counter.

Abigail glared for a moment, but didn't lash out. Eventually she calmly said, "I didn't hurt Jane. I'm trying to find out what happened to her. She was my friend, Lilly. I joined the book club quite soon after I moved here, and I am very upset about what happened to her. All I'm doing is trying to find out what happened to my friend."

Lilly was sad to realise she still didn't believe Abigail was being sincere. The way she'd tried to take a picture of Jane's dead body had been callous in the extreme. It was difficult to believe she had any genuine friendships at all.

"I saw in your notes you were writing about Elizabeth Davenport. I can't imagine what sort of motive she would have."

"I thought the same thing at first. Elizabeth certainly wouldn't have wanted her party ruined," Abigail said. "She's all about reputation and standing. But, I got a glimpse of Jane's phone during the book club meeting and there were some rather alarming messages from Elizabeth warning Jane not to embarrass her in front of Lady Gresham."

"When did you go through her phone?"

"After she was found dead. My first instinct was to go through her bag before the police got there to try to find a clue. I sneaked away for a minute while we were all waiting."

Lilly then remembered Abigail had disappeared immediately after she had stopped her from photographing the scene.

"What did you find out?"

"I looked at her text history and found a conversation between her and Elizabeth," Abigail said, grabbing her own phone from her bag. "I took some pictures. Here, look."

Now that Abigail was in a sharing mood to prove she was innocent, she was happy to let Lilly see her phone. The text read;

> **ELIZABETH**: *Just a word of warning you better watch that vicious mouth of yours today*
> **JANE**: *?*
> **ELIZABETH**: *Don't act as though you don't know what I'm talking about*
> **JANE**: *I don't*
> **ELIZABETH**: *Honestly! After the way you acted in front of Lady Defoe you are lucky to get an invitation at all*
> **JANE**: *Don't be so dramatic*
> **ELIZABETH**: *I'm not being dramatic. You were childish and mean and you'd better watch what you say today in front of Lady Gresham*
> **JANE**: *I've already apologised*
> **ELIZABETH**: *It makes no difference. What I want is to be able to move on so don't you dare act that way again and try to embarrass me in front of my friends or you will be sorry*
> **JANE**: *Such a drama queen like always, Elizabeth*

"Good grief! They were on worse terms than I thought," Lilly said.

"Exactly. They were at one another's throats the entire time during the discussion about the book too, because Jane contradicted something Elizabeth said and she in turn was mortified about how Meredith Gresham was viewing the whole discussion and her in particular. It was thinly veiled snipes almost from start to finish."

"I can't understand why she invited Jane in the first place, if they felt like this about one another. Have you told the police you've got this?"

"Not yet, but I will. They took Jane's bag and phone, so I expect they've found the texts by now."

"Well, you may be onto something here, you know?" Lilly said.

"Of course I am," Abigail said, with no modesty at all. She put her phone and notebook back in her bag. "I think Elizabeth had a motive. For all we know, she planned the whole book club meeting just so she could get Jane into her house to kill her."

"In revenge? Do you not think that would be a little far-fetched? I mean, at a tea party there would surely be easier ways to murder someone. She could have poisoned the tea for one thing."

"What and let you get the blame? I don't think so, Lilly. Besides you were the only one in charge of the pots and the brewing. You brought all your own cups as well. I don't think she'd have been able to do that without being seen. But I do think revenge could have been on her mind."

"Yes, I suppose you have a point there. It wouldn't have worked that way, thank goodness."

"No. But it was a messy way to do it, wasn't it? Whoever the murderer was, they were extremely fortunate not to get covered in blood. That would have been an immediate giveaway."

"It's easy than you think actually, as she was attacked from behind and very quickly. So, you know all these women fairly well, Abigail?"

She nodded. "I've been part of the book club for quite a while now."

"If you don't mind me saying so, you don't really seem to fit the mould for the type of woman Elizabeth Davenport... well..."

Abigail laughed, sounding almost friendly. "You mean I don't seem to fit into her little collection of titled and wealthy?"

"Yes, I suppose I do, although I wasn't going to describe them in quite that way."

"It's true. Elizabeth is a collector. Her favourite thing to collect is people, odd as it sounds. She doesn't so much make friends as add them to her group as a way of adding interest to herself. Me? I was the new agony aunt at the newspaper. A professional woman who was part of a large and well-known national company. I was established and my name was recognised with my former paper, so she invited me along when I first moved here. I think she initially thought I was going to be quite famous here too then it all turned out... well not quite how I expected. She ignored me for some time after; until I wrote that front page article with Archie, then suddenly I was her best friend again. It's obvious she thinks that by making important connections she in turn will be made to look important. Not that I'd ever accuse her to her face. I'd be on her radar like Jane and Isadora before I could say old news."

Lilly frowned. "I understand Elizabeth's confrontation with Jane, but what do you mean about Isadora being on her radar?"

"Oh, didn't you know? It is one-upmanship and competition just about all the time with those two. I've just told you Jane annoyed her intensely at the meeting, but you should have heard Isadora. She put a lot of work into sounding smart and ingenious in front of Lady Gresham, cleverer than her host especially. She and Elizabeth are always trying to outdo and outshine each other," Abigail explained. "It's just the way they are. If I'm honest, one of the main reasons I attend these functions is because they're a huge source of entertainment. I hardly ever read the books."

Lilly laughed.

"Well, Lilly, I need to leave. Thank you for the tea and for letting me clean up," Abigail said, picking up her bag and exciting through the back door.

Lilly watched her leave. Earl let out a small meow and Lilly absently scratched his ears. "Do you know, Earl, that was almost civil towards the end. If only she made a bit more of an effort, then I'm sure she would make more friends and become better at her job. I wonder what her story really is?"

Chapter Nine

*T*HE NEXT MORNING, while Stacey and Lilly were busy in the shop, a special delivery arrived. It was the tea set that Elizabeth Davenport had ordered.

"Hey, Lilly," Stacey said, as she'd been the one to greet the driver. "It looks like that second fancy tea set has arrived."

"Perfect," Lilly said, as Stacey set the large box on the counter for her to inspect. "I had hoped it would arrive at the same time Lady Defoe's did, considering they were ordered on the same day. But never mind."

Lilly opened the box and carefully took out each piece to ensure there were no cracks or chips or full-blown breakages which had occurred in transit. Everything was perfect, so she carefully wrapped and repackaged it all, ready to take to its new owner.

"Okay, that's all fine, let's get it wrapped in The Tea Emporium gift wrap and I'll drive over and deliver it."

"Do you always make home deliveries when orders arrive?" Stacey asked.

"I try to. If it's something small that I can fit in my bicycle basket and for someone who lives close by, I'll bike over."

"But this is neither. Mrs Davenport lives miles away, and it's too big for your bike."

"Yes, that's true, but it's a beautiful set and one of the most expensive I have to offer. Something like this deserves a special delivery. If the customer lives in Plumpton Mallet, I usually try to make a personal delivery, even if it means taking the car. It brings back repeat custom if they have a good experience."

"And it gives you a chance to ask Mrs Davenport some more questions about what happened at the book club meeting," Stacey teased. Lilly had already brought Stacey up to date with everything that had happened, including the incident and subsequent conversation with Abigail the evening before. In typical Stacey fashion she had turned the whole thing into a running joke, constantly asking Lilly whether she was setting up as a private investigator and if she was attempting to ruin Abigail's life and car in the process. She finished by saying if Abigail was forced to dye her hair black to disguise the paint, then it wouldn't matter if she lost her job, because she could make loads of money standing in for Cruella de Vil. Lilly had had to pass that little gem on to Archie, who laughed uproariously. Luckily Jim had been true to his word and there was no sign of the mess outside the shop now. What Abigail looked like was another thing entirely.

"Well, yes, there is that too," Lilly now said. "Could you help me put this in my car so I can deliver it today?"

"Sure."

They shut the shop for five minutes while they traipsed back and forth through the storeroom to the car park with the boxes, and very carefully put them in the boot.

"It seems to me like the more expensive the china, the more delicate and breakable it is," Stacey said, as they loaded the last of the boxes.

"That's absolutely right. Fine porcelain like these are fired at a higher temperature and will allow bright light to pass through. But because of the firing method, they are much more expensive to produce. The downside is despite its strength, it does chip more easily. When I first opened, I felt as though I was having to replace something every other day. It took me some time to get used to the fact that no matter how excited I was to see the new stock, I shouldn't rush to unbox it, otherwise I'd ruin all my merchandise. Now, are you okay to run the shop for a while if I make this delivery now?"

"Absolutely fine, don't worry," Stacey assured her, so Lilly got in the car and drove out of town to the Davenport home.

It was the first time Lilly had been back to Elizabeth's house since Jane had died, and it brought back an eerie sense of deja vu as she made her way down the drive. The gates, once again, had been opened by some unknown method.

She parked and went up the steps and was about to knock on the door, when it was opened by Elizabeth Davenport.

"Lilly, how lovely to see you again, please tell me my gorgeous tea set has arrived and you're here to deliver it?"

"Got it in one,"

"Fabulous," she said, following Lilly to help carry the boxes into the house. "I told my husband that I had a charming little tea set coming. He thinks I spent too much, of course, but I believe when he sees the design and the superb quality he'll agree it was worth it. I intend to have an afternoon tea for him this week to show it off."

Lilly followed Elizabeth through to her kitchen and they chatted while they gently unpacked. It was a set of tea cups and saucers, Teapot, side plates and various accessories. "This is all so wonderful," Elizabeth said, holding a cup up to the light. "And thank you for delivering it, you didn't have to."

"I wanted to. A special tea service deserves a special delivery."

"It's kind of you, dear. What can I say? I have a refined taste."

Perhaps because of Stacey's teasing earlier, or possibly the result of being back where the murder took place, Lilly had a sudden, alarming thought. She'd just remembered that during the course of conversation at her demonstration, Elizabeth had mentioned having a hatpin collection to rival that of Isadora's! With the shock of the murder, she'd completely forgotten about it. She needed more information. Anything she could gather for Bonnie was sure to help, especially as the police were now working on the hatpin angle.

"You most certainly do, Elizabeth. You definitely have a skill for identifying good quality." Elizabeth Davenport positively preened. "In fact, I wonder if you would mind giving me some advice on hatpins? I remember you said you had a lovely collection when I remarked on Isadora's. It piqued my interest. Do you think I could see it?"

"Oh, you're thinking about starting a collection too? You won't be disappointed. They are so very interesting and quite beautiful. Some plain and some ornate, but all with such lovely history. I always wonder what sort of woman would have worn the ones I now have. Come along and see." She beckoned Lilly to follow and led her through to the drawing room where a display cabinet on ornate legs was filled with a small, unique collection of trinkets, including several hatpins.

"Goodness, how lovely," she said, admiring the sparkling items. She noted the case appeared to be locked, but there was some damage to the surrounding wood. "Oh dear, did something happen to the case?"

"It's been like that for a few days," Elizabeth said with a huff. "I'm not sure what happened to it. It's quite aggravating because it ruins the look, doesn't it? My husband has been promising to fix it, but he's a businessman rather than a handy man, I'm afraid. I think I'm going to have to call in a professional to see to it. I do so hate to see it looking this way, it rather spoils things don't you think?"

Lilly nodded. "Well, your collection is lovely." She looked at all the hatpins, noting the display didn't appear to have a gap where something was missing. Of course, it would have been easy enough for Mrs Davenport to rearrange the items to hide the space. "Would you mind if I used your cloakroom before I left?"

"Not at all, you go ahead. I was going to make some tea to break in the new set. Would you like to join me?"

"That would be lovely, thank you. I never turn down a cup of tea."

"Neither do I. It's always teatime here at the Davenport's."

Lilly headed to the bathroom as Elizabeth returned to the kitchen. The whole place had been thoroughly cleaned since Jane had been found, and there was no sign at all of the tragedy that had occurred. Lilly took her time scouring every inch of the place anyway, even though she knew it was unlikely she'd find anything helpful. She was feeling discouraged when she re-entered the hall, then for a split second, as the sun shone through the glass panel in the front door, a brief sparkle caught her eye. It came from a large pot housing a huge potted palm in the entrance foyer. She approached and leaned down, reaching into the pot, and gasped. She pulled out a diamond encrusted jewel in the shape of a letter E, a snapped stem at the back. It was the missing decorative end of the hatpin! "E for Elizabeth..." she breathed, realising the woman must have commissioned a personalised hatpin for herself.

Lilly didn't waste any time and darted back into the cloak-room to hide from Elizabeth, the missing part of the murder weapon still in her hand, and called Bonnie. When she informed her what she'd found, Bonnie told her to remain in the cloakroom and wait for her arrival. She was on her way immediately. Under no circumstances was she to let anyone at all know what she'd found. And that included Elizabeth Davenport.

A moment later there was a knock on the cloakroom door and Elizabeth called out. "Are you all right, Lilly? The tea is nearly ready. I thought we'd have it on the patio?"

"Yes, I'm fine. That sounds lovely," Lilly called out. "I'll be there in a moment."

Almost immediately, she heard the doorbell. Bonnie must have either driven like a rally driver, or more likely been quite close to Dovecote Grange already when Lilly had called her. Or it was someone else entirely. "Oh, there's someone at the door, dear, I won't be a minute."

She heard raised voices muffled behind the closed cloakroom door, followed by an insistent knock. "You all right, Lilly?" Bonnie asked.

"Fine," she said, opening the door and showing her the broken hatpin she'd found only moments before.

Bonnie took it carefully and nodded. "Yes, that's definitely a match. I don't suppose you thought about fingerprints?"

"Oh, Bonnie! No, I never thought. I just grabbed it and called you. I'm so sorry."

"Doesn't matter, hopefully we'll get something from it."

"Where's Mrs Davenport?" Lilly asked.

"In the back of the car, in cuffs, she's protesting her innocence, of course. She'll be taken to the station and questioned. Well done, Lilly."

Lilly nodded. "I'll just go and check everything's all right in the kitchen. I'd hate for her to have left the kettle boiling away on the cooker top and burn the place down."

THE NEXT MORNING, the front page of The Plumpton Mallet Gazette carried the story of Elizabeth Davenport's arrest for the murder of Jane Nolan. It had been written by Abigail Douglas and was sensationalism at its finest. Lilly found this surprising considering Archie had only recently told her the bosses at the paper didn't want Abigail anywhere near the Jane Nolan story. Either she'd pitched something so compelling to the editors that they were willing to overlook her involvement and conflict of interest, or now that someone had been arrested for the crime she'd been let off the hook.

Lilly stood on the pavement outside her shop reading the article and shaking her head. It wasn't that it was badly written. Compared to Abigail's recent articles it actually was a vast improvement, but the entire thing was full of speculation and assumptions that a half decent reporter would have either worded differently or most likely, omitted. Of course, the word 'allegedly' was sprinkled liberally throughout to avoid getting the paper into serious trouble and on the wrong end of a lawsuit. Even so, the tone was highly accusatory, and Lilly found herself quite offended by it. She was surprised the chief editor had given the go ahead for it to be printed.

"I can't believe it," she muttered, shaking her head and folding the paper in half, tucking it under her arm. She leaned down and picked up the watering can she'd abandoned after discovering the paper tucked under one of the plant pots. She watered the plants, tall red geraniums surrounded by a waterfall of delicate blue, pink and purple lobelia that decorated her bike and returned inside.

Stacey was busy assisting a customer who was trying to choose a new tea, selecting sample after sample in an attempt to find the perfect blend. After returning the watering can to its place in the cupboard and setting the newspaper down by the till, Lilly took the selected leaves from Stacey and offered to brew a pot. "I think you'll really like this one," Stacey said to the young man. "I'm a huge fan of all the Chamomile teas, but this one is the absolute best."

"Thanks," he replied. "I've been feeling a bit stuck in my ways recently and decided it's time I tried something new. My mum always made mint tea, so it was something I grew up with, but I'm just discovering there's so much more to try."

"I've been expanding my own palate a lot since I started working here," Stacey said while they waited for the tea to brew. "I'm from the states, which you can probably tell from my accent. I spent most of my time in the south where their tea is pretty much just black, iced and filled with sugar."

Both Lilly and the young customer wrinkled their noses. "Sounds dreadful," he said.

"I ought to make you a southern belles sweet tea sometime, Lilly," Stacey offered with a huge grin.

"Please don't," Lilly said, and the three of them laughed just as the tea was ready to pour. Truth be told, Lilly was usually willing to try just about any type of tea, but black iced tea sweetened with so much sugar was just too much. Not to mention her teeth probably wouldn't thank her for it as James Pepper had said.

Stacey poured each of them a beverage, using the vintage mix-matched cups Lilly kept on display behind the counter. She smiled when Stacey handed hers over in the new teacup she'd bought from Rosie's antique shop. Stacey knew Lilly had wanted to try it out. Luckily it didn't leak, which had been Lilly's main worry.

"Wow," the young man said when he took a healthy mouthful. "This is excellent. Okay, you've sold it to me. I'll have a large box, please."

Stacey rang his order up and he departed with words of thanks and promises to be back, leaving Lilly and Stacey alone in the shop. "Been kind of slow this morning," Stacey said. "He's only the fifth customer we've had. It's weird how random the influx of customers is round here. You can't keep track of it."

"Don't worry, I'm sure it will pick up soon." Lilly said with confidence. "Mid week is always slower, while the end of the week and the weekend is always busier because of the extra buses full of tourists that turn up."

Stacey picked up the newspaper Lilly had left by the till, reading the front page with interest. "You told me about the police taking away Mrs Davenport," she said, speed reading the article with a frown. "It's a bit judgmental, isn't it? It's as though she's already been found guilty."

"I know," she said, wondering what Stacey's thoughts were. Stacey had no journalism experience and was young, probably not an avid news reader, but even she could see the blatant faults in the article after only a brief read. She was interested in her take on it all. "All the evidence found was circumstantial. Even though the decorative E on the hatpin was a little telling."

"Yeah, but, Lilly, it's too obvious. I mean, that just tells you who it belonged to not who used it. And would Mrs Davenport use the only one that she could be linked to like that?" Stacey shook her head. "Ever since you told me what happened at her house yesterday, I've been thinking about it. That broken bit you found was stashed in a plant pot after one of the women, supposedly Elizabeth Davenport, stabbed and killed Jane Nolan. They washed up in the cloakroom sink and then we're supposed to believe they ditched the broken part in a pot and left it there, right?"

"Right."

"But I was thinking, if it was Mrs Davenport, why would she leave the murder weapon in the plant? She *lives* there. Jane was killed days ago, so that means she's spent all this time in her own house knowing the key piece of evidence that could pin, sorry that wasn't meant as a joke, the key piece of evidence that could *connect* her to the murder, was sitting right there a couple of metres from the crime scene. She had plenty of time to go and remove it and dispose of it somewhere else. Somewhere better, where no one would *ever* find it. Instead she chose to leave it there, knowing sooner or later someone would be bound to come across it? That's all kinds of stupid, Lilly, and Mrs Davenport doesn't strike me as being that much of an idiot."

Lilly nodded. "I agree with everything you've said and have been thinking along those lines myself. If she is the guilty party, then it wasn't the wisest move. Unless she's double bluffing, but I don't think that's the case at all. Elizabeth Davenport is far from stupid."

"That's what I'm saying. If she did it, then she'd have got rid of the letter E part of the murder weapon as soon as she could. It makes me think she couldn't possibly have known it was there. Which means she isn't the one to have killed Jane at all. I'm pretty sure the police are going to figure that one out too before long, if they haven't already. I bet they're annoyed they didn't find the head of that pin."

"I agree," Lilly said. "But, just to play devil's advocate here, Elizabeth cares very deeply about her reputation. Jane put a not inconsiderable dent in it, in front of a lot of people she called her friends, and Elizabeth was both angry and mortified. But, would she really have risked her reputation and standing in the community by committing murder? The scandal would have been off the charts in a small town like this. Well, it is now actually since the article came out."

"Mm, maybe, but not this way," Stacey said.

"What do you mean?"

"I mean, I don't really know this woman or anything, but it seems to me if she was going to commit murder she wouldn't have done it like this. She would have made a good plan. She acts like a planner, you know? Like the day she ordered the exact same tea set on the exact same day as Lady Defoe happened to be here. I think she knew Lady Defoe was coming. It was her first time here, remember, and planned to be in the shop just before she arrived so she could accidentally bump into her."

"Actually, that's more than possible. I've learned all these women play little games like this. But planning to bump into someone is a far cry from planning to bump them off, Stacey."

"Yeah, well, I still don't think she did it," she said, getting up and stretching her back. "It's all a bit too convenient. Which means one of those ladies she calls her friends has set her up!"

"Yes, I know. And sadly, I believe you're right."

"Okay, well, there was a bunch of deliveries came in yesterday, so I need to go through the boxes and get the teas organised in the back. Since there are no customers in right now, do you mind if I go ahead and make a start?"

"No, that would be great. I'll watch the shop and let you know if I need you."

*L*ILLY DECIDED TO use the uncommonly quiet time to go through her accounts. She gathered the receipts and her ledger and set to work, sitting at the counter with a freshly made cup of ginger and honey tea, needing the boost to her brain. She preferred to do things by hand initially, then transfer it all into her accounting software. She'd been caught out before when her laptop had died, taking with it all her accounts information. It had been several days before she could find someone to fix it and retrieve the information. She wouldn't be caught out again. She'd been working for a couple of minutes when Earl left his spot in the window and jumped into her lap. For a former stray, he'd certainly adapted to domesticated life quickly.

She'd hardly put pen to paper when she was interrupted a second time. This time it was the phone.

"Hello, Archie. You're calling to complain about a certain Ms Douglas, I take it?"

"You saw the article then?"

"I did. It wasn't good, was it? How did it get the go ahead, Archie?"

"The chief editor made a bad call on that one," he said. "You should have seen the original version Abigail turned in, though. It stated Elizabeth Davenport was the murderer no question, even though she hasn't even been charged yet. She's just in for questioning under caution from what I understand while the police gather all the evidence. She was told to fix it and what you read was the result. I think he only approved it because we were so close to the deadline, and he's already regretting the decision. He's been stuck in his office with the phone ringing off the hook all morning. There's been complaints from several quarters, not least from Mr Davenport, who is absolutely furious and threatening to sue. I can't blame him I'd do the same thing if I was in his shoes."

"Well, if it's any consolation, I though the writing itself was much improved. I even detected your voice in some places."

"I've been teaching her as you suggested. She's a pretty good pupil actually, until she decides that she knows best, which is most of the time, unfortunately. She's ruining everything, Lilly."

"I'm sorry, Archie, I know how much you care about the paper's reputation. We all should, it's been around for years and is as much a part of the town as the church or the town hall. The chief should have put you in charge of the story until Abigail was ready."

"Isn't hindsight a wonderful thing," Archie sighed heavily. "If they keep letting Abigail run wild like this, then I have no doubt the paper will turn into a gutter rag, or worse have to fold. It's already a laughingstock. I think for some reason they're afraid of sacking her. She came from the big suits side of things during the merger and has connections we don't have. I've told him to start documenting every single screw up, no matter how small, so when the time comes he'll have the proof he needs to get rid of her once and for all."

"You don't think that's a bit over the top, Archie?"

"Absolutely not!"

"So, what are your thoughts about Elizabeth Davenport being the murderer?" she asked, eager to change the subject. Abigail Douglas was going to cause Archie to have a stroke one of these days.

"Nonsense," he said immediately. "Jane Nolan embarrassing her once in public is not a motive for murder. It's ludicrous. And her hiding the weapon in her own home and leaving it there? It makes no sense."

"Stacey and I were just saying the same thing," she said, just as the shop door opened. "I've got to go, Archie, I've got a customer. Chin up, my friend, it will all work out, and I'm here when you need your dose of tea and sympathy."

"Thanks, Lilly. Talk to you later."

She ended the call and lifted Earl onto the counter, just as Fred Warren walked in.

"Hi, Lilly."

"Good morning, Fred. Do you want me to let Stacey know you're here? She's in the back."

"Actually, I'm looking for your help," He said, lifting a brown paper bag. "I have a broken teacup and Stacey told me you do repairs?"

"I do. Bring it over to the repair station and I'll see what I can do."

She unrolled the thick red velvet cloth and plugged in her magnifying light. Taking the cup from Fred, she placed it on the cloth and inspected it closely.

"It belonged to my Grandma, part of a set and mum's really upset about it. But Stacey said you were a miracle worker with this sort of thing."

The cup was obviously old and not in good shape. There were two cracks running its full length and a missing v-shaped chip from the rim. The delicate handle also had a small chunk missing from the bottom. She switched off her light and turned to Fred. "It will definitely be a challenge, but I believe I can repair it. It will take some time as it's neither easy nor quick, but I think I can make it look almost as good as new."

"Brilliant!" Fred said. "Doesn't matter how long it takes, mum just wants it back in one piece and looking like the rest."

The shop door opened again, and Lilly glanced up to see James Pepper walk in.

Chapter Ten

*L*ILLY'S GAZE WENT from James to Fred, then back again. James walked up to the counter paying Fred no attention and addressed Lilly. "Good morning," he said in his friendliest tone. "Is Stacey in?"

She saw Fred glance in James' direction. "She's working in the back at the moment. There are a few deliveries to unpack and put away, but she shouldn't be too long."

"Thank you, Lilly."

"How have you been, James?" Lilly asked, keen to keep the equilibrium going.

"Quite well. I've been staying at a nice hotel just out of town. It's been lovely staying in Plumpton Mallet in between summer courses."

"Ah, so the universities in London are taking a break at the moment?" Lilly asked pleasantly, and the question evidently caught Fred's attention. She assumed Stacey had told him her father taught at a London university, but she'd confessed she was uncomfortable with the two of them meeting just yet. Lilly suspected her father being so far away had been a good excuse to avoid an introduction. *And now here they are, both together in my shop*, Lilly thought.

"How do you know Stacey?" Fred asked pleasantly, now his suspicions had been raised, and Lilly cringed, wishing she'd never asked about the university.

James shot him an annoyed glance. "I'm her father."

Fred went quiet and turned away to avoid eye contact. James stared for a moment, but before he could question the boy's strange behaviour Stacey came back into the shop.

"Hey, Lilly, I've finished with the unpacking, but..." she froze when she saw the two men standing together at the counter.

"Thank you, Stacey." Lilly said.

"Hi, babe," Fred muttered, and James' eyebrows disappeared into his hairline.

Lilly felt as though she were watching a soap opera, or more aptly an American sitcom. She turned the light on and went back to studying Fred's damaged cup. She didn't want to appear to be eavesdropping, but she wanted to be within easy reach if things became heated.

"Did you two meet?" Stacey asked awkwardly.

Fred shook his head. "No, he's just arrived."

"Right. Well..." Stacey said, taking a deep breath. "Fred, this is my dad. Dad, I didn't know you were coming by today?"

James Pepper nodded, turning to Fred. "And you are?"

"I'm Frederick Warren, Mr Pepper," he said, sticking out his hand. "I'm Stacey's boyfriend."

James hesitated for a second, then shook the proffered hand. "Nice to meet you, Frederick. Then turned back to his daughter. "I came to bring you the application for London."

"Huh?" Stacey asked, confused.

It was then that Lilly noticed the file tucked under James' arm, which he passed to Stacey. "You'll see I've already written you a letter of recommendation, but feel free to review it. With that and your impressive grades, there's a very high chance you'll be accepted." He looked at Fred for a moment, then turned back to Stacey. "I hope having a boyfriend here won't interfere with your decision to pursue a better educational opportunity?"

Stacey opened the folder and briefly read the contents before laughing and putting it on the counter. "Why didn't you talk to me about this before spending time writing a recommendation, dad?"

James folded his arms, annoyed. Clearly he had expected gratitude as opposed to hilarity. "I beg your pardon?"

"If you'd asked me, I would have told you I wasn't interested in attending your school. I mean, don't get me wrong, studying in London would be an awesome opportunity for the right person, but I've got plans for my future and London isn't part of them."

"Stacey," James Pepper countered. "Plumpton Mallet is a small town with minimal opportunities. It has a reasonably good university, but it pales in comparison to London. With a degree from London you could..."

"Do you even know what I'm studying?" Stacey interrupted, becoming a bit annoyed.

James obviously didn't know the answer. "Well..." he began, but Stacey cut him off again.

"It's not on the curriculum where you teach, dad, so would never be part of my plan. And, since you don't know and have never bothered to ask, I'll tell you; I'm majoring in sports science. My goal is to become a physical sports therapist. And, guess what? St John's University, here in this small town, has one of the best programs in the country." She softened her voice. "Dad, I didn't reach out to you because of your connections, or to attend a London university. I never needed you to do that for me. I reached out because I wanted you, my father, to be part of my life. I thought we could at last get to know each other properly."

James Pepper was completely lost for words. Part of Lilly was relieved to hear that Stacey would not be leaving for London after all, but the other part felt rather sorry for James. He obviously believed he was putting his daughter first for once, but now he didn't know what to either say or do.

"James, perhaps you'd like to visit St John's? See what the university has to offer. Take a tour," she said, looking at Stacey and getting an encouraging nod. "I'm sure Stacey would love to show you around and tell you about the program she's studying. With your background, I expect you'll have a lot in common with the professors there and they would welcome an exchange of knowledge. Perhaps you might even know some of them?"

James slowly nodded in response, "Actually, I'd enjoy that," giving Lilly a brief smile of thanks. "Stacey, would you be willing to show your old dad around the place?"

"Yeah, sure, that'd be great. I get off at five, maybe we could get dinner?"

"Yes, we can do that," he turned to Fred. "Nice to meet you, Frederick." Then, with a final nod to everyone, he left.

"I can't believe your dad tried to get you to change schools without even knowing what you were studying," Fred said. "That was weird."

"That's my dad for you," Stacey said. "Sorry, Fred, I didn't plan on you meeting him like that the first time."

"He seems okay," Fred said with a smile. "I mean, he did all that work to try to help you, even if it wasn't what you wanted. You know, his intentions were good."

"Yeah, I guess."

Lilly's phone buzzed as Stacey and Fred continued to talk together at the end of the counter. It was a message from Archie asking her if she had time for lunch. She messaged back to confirm.

"Stacey, that was Archie asking if I could meet him for lunch. Will you be okay to hold the fort here for an hour or so?"

"Yeah, of course. I'll get Fred to do some dusting," she laughed.

"That's fine by me," Lilly said.

"Well, I hope you're insured, Miss Tweed, my mum says I have butter fingers."

"Ah," Lilly said, looking at the broken teacup.

Fred nodded. "Yep, why do you think I'm so keen to get it mended?"

"In that case, I think Stacey needs to find you something else to do if you're planning on staying for a while."

"No problem, there's lots of stuff needs doing in the store-room which doesn't involve delicate items. Don't worry, Lilly."

"All right, in that case it's all yours. I'll pick you both up some lunch on the way back. Anything in particular?"

Fred and Stacey looked and each other then both said, "Pizza!"

Lilly laughed. "Pizza it is. I know I don't have to tell you, but please keep it professional while I'm out."

❦

*L*ILLY TOOK HER bike to the pub where she had arranged to meet Archie in the small beer garden at the back. It was a place familiar to them both, as it was where they used to go for lunch, if their schedules allowed, when she'd worked at the paper. She wheeled her bike through the side entrance to the garden and got a strange sense of déjà vu when she spotted Archie at the back table underneath a tree. It was like stepping back in time, as though they were about to discuss office politics and deadlines as opposed to two friends catching up. She leaned her bike against the tree and took a seat opposite. Archie had already ordered drinks and lunch for them both, and when they were delivered to the table, they spent a few minutes talking about her shop and other things before the conversation drifted to Elizabeth Davenport.

"I spoke with her husband this morning," Archie said.

"Oh? How is he?"

"He's furious about the article as you'd expect, but he's absolutely adamant his wife is innocent, and he's worried things are going to go wrong for her very quickly if the real culprit isn't found. He seems to believe the police have stopped trying to find anyone else now they have his wife in custody. Poor man is really going through the wringer."

Lilly nodded, finishing a mouthful of chicken salad. "I'm not surprised. The so called evidence is all circumstantial at best. What are his thoughts about it being Elizabeth's hatpin that was used as the murder weapon?"

"The police have told him a hatpin was the murder weapon and that they believe it belonged to his wife, but he doesn't know which one. They're playing it close to their chests at the moment. He did admit that he probably wouldn't recognise it anyway. He doesn't take a lot of notice of his wife's collections. Just lets her get on with it if it makes her happy."

Lilly nodded. "Bonnie made me swear not to tell anyone exactly what I'd found, too. Unfortunately, I let it slip to Stacey. But she's promised not to breathe a word, and I trust her to keep her promise. Did Mr Davenport say anything else?"

"Yes. He said anyone could have taken it and stabbed Jane. It was on public display to all those who ventured into the drawing room, and the display case had been tampered with. He also pointed out that as his wife had the key, she wouldn't have needed to break it open."

"He makes a good argument," Lilly said. "And I really can't see her damaging her own furniture. When I visited her, she was genuinely upset about the damage. She's very house proud, you know."

"The police thought perhaps Mr Davenport was so desperate to prove his wife's innocence that he broke into the cabinet himself to point the finger at it being someone else. Which I suppose is feasible, but I doubt it."

"No, he didn't do that," Lilly said, shaking her head. "It was already damaged when I was there, which was just before I found the missing piece of the hatpin. I saw it myself. Elizabeth told me it had been broken for a few days. It's what we've all been thinking, you, me and Stacey. Someone else murdered Jane Nolan and threw the end of the hatpin in the plant pot in a panic, not expecting it to snap, maybe? And possibly with the thoughts of going back and retrieving it once things had settled down."

"The police will side with the Davenport's eventually, they have to," said Archie. "There are too many holes and not enough evidence in the case against her."

"Which means Jane's killer is still out there. Maybe it's time I spoke with Mr Davenport myself."

Just as Archie was downing the last of his pint, he received a text. "Oh well, duty calls. I've got to get back to the office, Lilly."

"Oh dear, not more crime?"

He shook his head. "No, it's some follow up pieces on Elizabeth Davenport and her life here in Plumpton Mallet. With no further news on the case, the boss wants to keep the momentum going with some background pieces. You know the sort of thing; old garden parties and charity events showing her rubbing shoulders with the town's elite."

"Yuck."

"Yes, but it sells papers. Lunch has been paid for by your old employer. Sorry to have to run."

"Don't worry about it. And thanks for lunch, we should try to do it more often. Bye, Archie."

Once Archie had left, Lilly sat alone for a while, deep in thought while she finished her apple juice. Then her phone rang.

"Hi, Bonnie, is everything all right?"

"I've just a bit of an update. Are you free for a chat?"

"Yes, of course. I've just finished having lunch with Archie, so I'm at the pub."

"Right, I'm on my way, see you in five minutes."

It was nearer ten when Bonnie put a glass of orange juice on the table and took a seat opposite Lilly.

"Bonnie, don't take this the wrong way, but you look awful. Are you all right?"

"Thank you for the boost to my confidence there, Lilly."

Lilly giggled. "I'm sorry. Is it the case?"

"The case, the whole case, and nothing but the case," Bonnie replied. "It's driving me to distraction that I'm putting in all these hours yet don't seem to be getting any further forward."

"Well, not getting enough sleep won't help. Drop by the shop and I'll mix you up a special tea blend. So what was it you wanted to tell me?"

"The end of the hatpin. Forensics have been studying it carefully and are now convinced, beyond a shadow of a doubt, that it was deliberately filed through to make sure the end snapped off when it was used to stab Jane Nolan."

"What?" Lilly said in astonishment. "But that makes no sense. Why would they do that?"

Bonnie shrugged. "Beats me, Lilly, nothing about this case makes sense to me so far."

"Well, what does Elizabeth Davenport say about it?"

"And that's the most mysterious part, Lilly. Elizabeth Davenport is adamant the hatpin is not hers."

⊗⊙⊙⊙

*L*ILLY DECIDED, AFTER her confusing conversation with Bonnie, there was no time like the present to visit Elizabeth's husband. After a brief text to Stacey letting her know of the changed plans, she said goodbye to Bonnie and set off to cycle to the Davenport's home.

It was a fairly long bike ride, but the weather was perfect, with the sun beating down from an azure sky and just enough of a cooling breeze to make the journey extremely pleasant. Her head was filled with thoughts of Elizabeth Davenport, currently sitting in a jail cell and probably extremely frightened. The whole experience must be dreadful for her, and now convinced of her innocence, Lilly was determined to prove it.

The gates opened automatically when she arrived, and wheeling the bike down the drive she saw an unfamiliar car. A top of the range deep bronze coloured Bentley in immaculate condition. *Probably Mr Davenport's* she thought. No doubt leaving it in a handy spot if he needed to get out quickly to see his wife or his solicitor.

She leaned her bike against the wall and ascending the front steps knocked loudly on the door. It was flung open a second later by a red faced harried looking gentleman. She had never met Mr Davenport before, but from the gossip around town she understood Elizabeth only dusted him off and took him to important events when she needed an arm to hang onto. He worked away a lot, so was hardly ever home. It seemed to her, Elizabeth filled her days with the likes of afternoon teas and book clubs to stave off the loneliness.

"May I help you," the man said now, making no attempt to conceal his irritation.

"Hello. Mr Davenport?" asked Lilly, just to make sure.

"Yes. Who are you? What do you want? You'd better not be from that damned paper."

"No, I'm not. My name is Lilly Tweed. I've..."

"You're the one who found that blasted hatpin!" He snapped, looking as though he wanted to push her down the steps. "What are you doing here? Thanks to you, I've been on the phone with the police and solicitors for the last twenty-four hours. Not to mention having to fend off those so called reporters. I was supposed to be leaving for an important business meeting this morning, but now I'm left dealing with this nightmare. Who do you think you are coming here? Don't you think you've caused enough trouble? My poor wife is currently languishing in a jail cell thanks to your interference. God only knows what it's doing to her mental health."

Lilly hadn't expected such a malevolent tirade and was a little nonplussed. "With all due respect, Mr Davenport," she began. "Yes, I found part of a murder weapon in your house and reported it to the authorities. It was not, however, with the intention of casting suspicion on your wife. You do realise that a young woman was savagely murdered in your cloakroom?"

Mr Davenport seethed for a moment, turning crimson, before taking several deep breaths in an attempt to calm down. "Yes, well, I apologise. This has been the worst twenty-four hours I've ever had."

"I'm sure it has been, and I'm terribly sorry for disturbing you again today, but I was hoping I could ask you about the relationship your wife had with Jane?"

"You and everyone else in this town," he said bitterly. "I'm going to tell you the same thing I told the police, Miss Tweed, Elizabeth had no reason and nothing to gain from hurting Jane Nolan. The so called evidence the police think they have is a joke. Anyone present that day could have taken that hatpin from the display, and if it had been my wife, she wouldn't have needed to break into her own cabinet to get it. Anyone with half a brain can see my wife has been made the scapegoat."

Lilly nodded. "I understand, Mr Davenport. And for what it's worth, I agree with you completely. I don't believe your wife murdered Jane. She doesn't have a solid motive for one thing."

"And Jane, of all people," the man continued not hearing Lilly's declaration, shaking his head in disbelief. "There are plenty of women my wife has clashed with, but that nasty little spat with Jane at the Defoe's would not have been enough for her to stab the woman to death. If she was that unhinged, and believe me she is not, I would have put my money on her getting rid of Isadora Smith."

"Isadora? Really? Why her?"

"Because after that particular incident Isadora deliberately poured salt onto the wound, she jumped on the bandwagon and continued to speak ill of Elizabeth to Lady Defoe. It made the situation a lot worse than it already was, and Elizabeth was hurt to the quick. I'm no fool, Miss Tweed, I know my wife better than anyone. Yes, she has snobbish tendencies and a wish to be seen in the best company and an almost childish desire to belong to the best circles. She's not particularly clever and her social skills aren't terribly subtle, but she is a good and kind person. Suffice to say Isadora, in my opinion, is not. Why Isadora's offensive behaviour was let slide and my Elizabeth cruelly picked on, I'll never know. But Isadora has always been a master of manipulation and has an innate ability to pull the wool over people's eyes so they don't recognise her spite for what it is. Personally, I think being sneaky and underhanded is far worse than being upfront."

"I had no idea," Lilly said. "I was informed that Lady Defoe gave Jane a dressing down for the way she'd treated Elizabeth that day. Did she not therefore scold Isadora too?"

"She did not. As I've just told you, Isadora is very subtle with her insults. Lady Defoe keeps her around because of her wit. She can be very amusing and entertaining, but she's one of the worst social climbers there is. Now, if you'll excuse me, I have several phone calls to make. I cannot let my wife squander in that cell a moment longer."

Mr Davenport shut the door and Lilly sloped back to her bike, deep in thought and feeling despondent. What had she really learned from that conversation? Naturally he would plead his wife's innocence, and Lilly agreed with him. But what about the rest? Was it all just sour grapes? Him grasping at straws in eagerness to point the finger at someone else? Isadora had been the only one who had greeted Lilly with anything remotely akin to friendliness. She'd found and returned her car keys when she'd dropped them. She'd also been honest and open about her spats with her friends, but had Lilly really been manipulated to the extent Mr Davenport had suggested Isadora was capable of? She didn't like to think of herself as being that gullible. She put the idea to the back of her mind and set off for the ride back to town, hoping she could unearth a real clue and a way forward very soon.

O N THE RETURN journey she suddenly remembered she had promised to pick up lunch for Stacey and Fred. Firing off a quick text to see if they still wanted something, she got a reply almost immediately in the affirmative and stopped at the Italian cafe on the outskirts of town, the best place for pizza. She ordered herself a cappuccino and sat at a free table in the corner behind a large plant while she waited for the pizza's to be made.

Her phone buzzed, indicating there was a text. Opening it, she found it was from Archie and it was marked urgent. Looking at her call history she'd realised he'd tried to phone her when she was cycling to the Davenport's but she hadn't heard it. She rang him back immediately.

"Archie, what is it?"

"I think I've just found the mother of all clues. I'm going to forward you some pictures from Lady Defoe's Easter garden party. We covered the event. See if you can spot what I did. Give me a call back as soon as you've seen them."

Lilly waited with bated breath for the images and pounced to open them the minute they arrived. At first she had no idea what Archie was getting at, it was images of the guests laughing, talking and drinking. She recognised a few of them; Lady Defoe obviously, her husband, the Gresham's, Jane, Isadora, Elizabeth. Mr Davenport standing alone by an Azalea bush nursing a glass of champagne and looking lost. Even Abigail was in a fair few of them. It wasn't until she read the text from Archie which accompanied each individual shot that she made the connection.

"Oh my god!" she breathed. She rang Archie back. "How did we miss it, Archie?"

"Well, how would we have known? She doesn't use that name, does she? I've spent every minute since you and I had lunch getting confirmation. I've called in every favour I had owing to me, and some I didn't. She hid it well. I doubt even her so-called friends know."

"Have you told Bonnie?"

"I'm just about to. She needs to go to the woman's house and see if she can find any other pins that would make up a set."

"She'll need more evidence, won't she, to be able to do a search?" asked Lilly.

"Possibly, but at least she can get the ball rolling based on that photo. It definitely counts as probable cause."

"Well done, Archie."

Lilly ended the call and continued to study the images. She now almost certainly knew the 'who', it was the 'why' she needed to work out. She looked up sharply when the door opened and she heard a voice she recognised.

"Oh, Theo, darling, I'm so glad you've not lost your sense of humour. It's so important to move on."

Lord Gresham and Isadora Smith and entered the cafe together. The casual flirtation caught Lilly's attention. Isadora was all batting eyelashes and smiles, Theodore much less so.

"I wasn't trying to be funny, Isadora," Theo said. "Why are we here? I would much rather have stayed at home. I haven't got much of an appetite, anyway."

"You needed to get out of the house," she replied, rubbing his arm. "And you must keep your strength up, Theo. I know you're still grieving, but staying inside and hidden away alone, is really not going to help. You needed some fresh air and a change of scenery. It will help you get out of this melancholy state of mind. It's not healthy, dearest."

Theo sighed deeply. "Yes, I suppose you're right. Thank you, Isadora."

Lilly had a good view of the pair but remained unnoticed by them. She studied them carefully. Isadora was standing much closer to her companion than necessary, and any excuse to lay a hand on his arm or stroke his shoulder, she took. She couldn't help but feel her behaviour was vulgar. It also wasn't being encouraged by Theo himself. The poor man had just lost the woman he had intended to make his wife, and while she didn't know this group of friends well, she thought Isadora was acting in poor taste. Theo seemed to expect it though, so perhaps it was typical Isadora behaviour. But the more she watched the interaction, the more she questioned Isadora's real motives.

Mr Davenport had suggested all the women to some extent were social climbers, but none more than Isadora Smith. Lilly also recalled the conversation she had had with Theo in Lady Defoe's garden. He commented on how concerned Isadora had been about him and had been checking up on him regularly. Even Isadora herself had told her she'd contacted him after Jane's death, and in tones that her affection for him was obvious.

A cold shiver suddenly went down Lilly's body and her heart began to thump. The pieces of the puzzle were at last beginning to come together. Had Isadora seized the opportunity to take out a romantic rival and frame Elizabeth Davenport in the process?

❦

*L*ILLY'S ORDER WAS ready and brought to her table by a bubbly waitress who caught the attention of Isadora and Theo. Their heads turned and Isadora locked eyes with Lilly.

"Oh, Lilly," Isadora called out from where they both stood holding take away coffee cups.

Lilly picked up her order and walked towards the couple. "Lord Gresham, Isadora," she greeted them with a forced smile.

"Have you heard the news, Lilly? Elizabeth Davenport has been arrested for Jane's murder! Isn't it simply dreadful?"

Isadora said, while Theo cringed next to her. Any mention of the case was naturally difficult for him.

"Yes, I have heard," Lilly replied. Then decided to see if she could get a reaction. "Although between you and me, the police are saying there's not sufficient evidence."

"Oh, really? I hadn't heard that. From the newspaper report it all seemed cut and dried to me."

"I have a friend working on the case," Lilly replied, matter-of-factly. Then decided to put the cat among the pigeons by coming up with a complete fabrication to see what the response would be. "But," she said, lowering her voice conspiratorially. The other two leaned in, wide eyed and expectant. "Between the three of us, they may have found additional evidence that points to someone other than Elizabeth Davenport as being the murderer."

Lord Gresham stood upright. "What additional evidence? And points to whom?"

"My friend couldn't say," Lilly said, watching Isadora fidget. "But apparently Mr Davenport had a new security system fitted recently and it included several discreet cameras around the house, one of which showed the front door and the cloakroom. Elizabeth was totally unaware they were switched on and recording the day of Jane's death. The police are reviewing it all now."

"Security cameras," Isadora whispered, looking extremely sick.

"Yes. By the end of today they should be able to confirm it wasn't Elizabeth who killed Jane."

"And who did," Lord Gresham said, sounding relieved and frightened in equal measure.

Lilly kept her eye on Isadora, hoping to see something that would confirm what she now knew to be true. Isadora was avoiding all eye contact and swaying. It seemed so obvious now and Lilly was annoyed she hadn't seen it sooner.

"Exactly, Lord Gresham. I think it will be very interesting to see what they find, don't you, *Isadora*?"

Theo caught Lilly's tone and emphasis immediately and turned quickly to his companion. "Isadora?" he said in puzzlement.

Isadora dropped her coffee and pushed through them both toward the door, hands raised. "I'm not... I'm not going to stand here and listen to this. You think I don't know what you're insinuating? It's repulsive. How dare you!"

"Isadora!" Theo shouted, in such an authoritative tone it startled her. She stopped inches from the door and turned to face him. "Did you kill Jane?"

Lilly took a step towards her. "I know it was you, Isadora. Or should I call you, Elsie?"

Isadora gasped, "No!"

"You wanted Jane out of the way so you could have Theodore all to yourself," Lilly continued. "As long as she was around he wouldn't look twice at you, isn't that right? So you seized the opportunity to kill Jane and aggressively pursue Theodore while he was at his lowest ebb. All while making sure Elizabeth got the blame. You used one of your own hatpins. One you had brought with you with the sole intention of using it to kill Jane that day at the book club meeting. That's premeditation. You have three, don't you? All part of an identical set using your initials. E I S. Elsie Isadora Smith."

"No, that's a lie. Don't listen to her, Theo, she's making it up."

"I have a picture of you wearing the letter 'I' in your hat on the day of Lady Defoe's Easter party, Isadora. It's identical to the letter 'E' that was used to kill Jane. Thanks to the skills of a superb investigative journalist, your full name has been confirmed. No doubt the police will find that 'I' and the letter 'S' when they search your home. And what's more, the police have discovered the letter 'E' was deliberately filed through so the end would easily snap when it was used. Allowing you to throw it in the plant pot where it would easily be found, incriminating Elizabeth."

"Is that what happened, Isadora? Did you take Jane's life just so you could have me?" Theo asked. He sounded shocked and incredulous. "The cameras will tell the truth, Isadora. So tell me now, did you do it?"

Isadora reached for the door. "You were too good for her," she cried, ready to bolt.

Lilly started to move, but Lord Gresham charged past her, reaching for Isadora. But she was too fast and out of the door before he could get there. He bolted outside, with Lilly quick on his heels. She made it outside in time to see Theo dive forward and rugby tackle Isadora to the ground. She hit the pavement hard.

"Help me!" he cried to Lilly, and she threw the pizzas on a nearby table and rushed to his aid, grabbing Isadora's left arm and pulling her to her feet.

"You're not going anywhere," she said. "We know you did it. It's over."

"Fine," Isadora screamed. "Good riddance to her, that's what I say."

"So you admit you killed Jane and tried to frame Elizabeth all so you could have Lord Gresham to yourself?"

"Yes, I killed her, and I don't regret a thing! You were going to throw your life away for that nasty mouthed trollop, Theo. I couldn't let you do it. You would have been happy with me."

Lilly pulled out her phone. Some sixth sense had told her to start recording the moment Isadora had spotted her in the cafe. "I've got her confession recorded."

"Between that, the photograph and the camera footage, the police will have an undisputed case against her," Theo said.

Lilly smirked. "What camera footage?"

Isadora's eyes widened at the realisation she'd been tricked, and Theo barked out a laugh.

"It serves you right, you monster!"

Lilly called the police and Isadora was promptly arrested for the murder of Jane Nolan, thanks to the statements and evidence she and Lord Gresham were able to provide.

Chapter Eleven

*L*ILLY WAS SITTING at the shop counter, a smile on her face as she read Archie Brown's latest newspaper article. Not only did it go into full detail about the investigation, including interviews of multiple witnesses, first-hand accounts of the murder and Isadora's arrest, but also included a wonderful correction notice and apology from the paper for Abigail's previous article.

"Reading Archie's article?" Stacey asked as she hurried past with a small box of handkerchiefs to put near the till. It was a new product one of Lilly's wholesalers had given her to try out in the shop. The handkerchiefs, superb quality silk in colours suitable for both men and women, had The Tea Emporium logo embroidered on one corner in gold thread. Lilly intended to give them away as a thank you gift for those whose orders were over a certain amount. Or they could be bought individually. But she doubted she'd include them in her range. They weren't quite in keeping with the ethos of her shop.

"How did you know?"

"By that big grin on your face," Stacey replied, laughing. "I read it earlier. It's great. You're mentioned by name again. You know what that means, don't you? You're going to get more customers in here wanting to meet the famous celebrity sleuth of Plumpton Mallet."

"I had thought that was going to die down," Lilly admitted, folding up the paper and putting it on the counter. "But I suppose this latest case has just re-lit the flame. Honestly though, I don't mind, it's been very good for business. But really Archie is the star of this one. He found the main the clue I just happened to be where Isadora was at the time."

"You think you're going to have any more trouble with Abigail over it?"

"I'm not sure, but I don't think so. Abigail and I reached a truce during that paint fiasco. I think she understands I am doing nothing to harm her reputation or risk her job. She's managing that quite well all by herself. The chief editor asking Archie to add the retraction notice was a bit harsh, I thought, though. Abigail didn't actually write anything that was blatantly untrue it was the tone that was wrong. However, I'm sure Mrs Davenport is relieved the gazette is attempting to right the error."

"She most certainly is!" Mrs Davenport's voice boomed across the shop as the door swung closed behind her.

Lilly rose from her seat while Stacey focused on arranging the new merchandise. "Elizabeth, welcome back, I'm so glad to see you walking out and about again."

"And it's all down to you, dear Lilly. I came by to thank you. I could have been in the most dreadful trouble if you hadn't pursued your own investigation and obtained Isadora's confession. I read the article this morning and thought it was so clever the way you did it, and had the brains to record it all too. It would never have occurred to me to do that. I must admit I am seriously considering having security cameras put up in my home, though. I never thought this dear little town could be so dangerous."

"I'm so relived you're not angry at me for calling the police in the first place when I found the rest of the hatpin in the plant pot."

"I won't deny that being in that cell was the worst experience of my life, Lilly. But you were doing what was right," Mrs Davenport said, patting Lilly's arm. "I certainly don't blame you for that. I'm sure I would have done the same thing had I been in your place. Even my husband said so."

"I'm glad to hear that. He wasn't very pleased to see me last time we spoke."

"It was worry and stress. He's not normally so abrupt. He's just glad I'm out of jail now. As am I. You did me a great service, Lilly Tweed."

Lilly shrugged. "It wasn't that much."

"You got a murderess to confess and clear my name. My good reputation, which means a lot to me, has been restored. And far from my horrible experience being a disaster, I have since been invited to tea by Lady Defoe. She's absolutely dying to hear all about it directly from me. She called it the story of the year when she telephoned."

Lilly smiled. She knew an invitation from Lady Defoe was a huge deal to Elizabeth Davenport and she was pleased for her.

"Just so you know, Lilly, you will be receiving my patronage, and that of Lady Defoe, a lot more in the future. She wants to hear all about your marvellous presentation. Take it from me I will be giving you a dazzling review. Now, my dear, if would be so kind, could you get me a box of Lady Defoe's favourite tea? I need to be sure I have it in next time she comes to visit."

Lilly watched happily as Elizabeth Davenport scurried out of the shop, head held high again and clutching two boxes of tea. She was still standing there when another familiar face entered. "Hello, James."

He nodded his head. "Lilly. I just came to say goodbye to Stacey before I head back to London."

"Hey, dad. You're leaving already?"

"I feel as though I may have overstayed my welcome in Plumpton Mallet," he said sadly.

"Is this because I told you I wouldn't be coming to London?"

"No, not really," although he sounded far from convincing.

Lilly made herself scarce while father and daughter continued their personal conversation. She decided to empty the agony aunt box. There were several letters, and she was busy outside the shop flipping through them when James exited. "Goodbye, Lilly. Hope to see you again soon." He certainly sounded happier.

"You too, James," she said, returning inside.

"Did that go well, Stacey?"

"I think so. I told him I knew he'd really tried with the letter and everything. And that I really appreciated the effort, but I needed him to stop trying to make up for the past. What I wanted was for him to get to know me *now*. For us both to get to know each other now, actually. I think the talk went well."

"I'm glad, Stacey. Hopefully you can both build a new relationship."

She was still holding the letters when Stacey asked, "What's that one? Doesn't look like the normal letters you get?"

She was right. Lilly opened it. "Oh, it's a wedding anniversary invitation. How lovely."

"Who from?"

"A few years ago, while I was still working at the paper, I received a letter from a widower. He was attracted to a widow but had been out of the dating game for so long he didn't know how to approach her. I wrote back giving him some advice."

"And?"

"And they've been married for nearly five years."

"And they want you to celebrate with them? That's so cool. You're going, right?"

"Well, it's out of town, what about the shop?"

"Lilly, I can handle it, you know I can."

"Well, I really could do with a holiday. And it's the south coast, a beautiful place where the sea is warm and with a private beach."

"You deserve a break after what you've been through these last few months. And I'll be on the other end of the phone. Earl will be very happy at my place, and it's a great excuse to hide from the busloads of tourists who are probably on their way right now to speak with the town's famous lady sleuth, thanks to this latest case."

"Do you know, Stacey, I think you've talked me into it."

"Great. Just relax and have fun. And stay well away from mysteries and murder."

Lilly laughed. "I doubt very much there'll be anything like that where I'm going."

If you enjoyed *A Deadly Solution*, book two in the Tea & Sympathy series, please leave a review on Amazon. It really does help and you'd make the author very happy.

ABOUT THE AUTHOR

J. New is the author of *THE YELLOW COTTAGE VINTAGE MYSTERIES,* traditional English whodunits with a twist, set in the 1930's. Known for their clever Humour as well as the interesting slant on the traditional murder mystery, they have all achieved Bestseller status on Amazon.

J. New also writes two contemporary cozy crime series:

THE TEA & SYMPATHY series featuring Lilly Tweed, former newspaper Agony Aunt now purveyor of fine teas at The Tea Emporium in the small English market town of Plumpton Mallet. Along with a regular cast of characters, including Earl Grey the shop cat.

THE FINCH & FISCHER series featuring mobile librarian Penny Finch and her rescue dog Fischer. Follow them as they dig up clues and sniff out red herrings in the six villages and hamlets that make up Hampsworthy Downs.

Jacquie was born in West Yorkshire, England. She studied art and design and after qualifying began work as an interior designer, moving onto fine art restoration and animal portraiture before making the decision to pursue her lifelong ambition to write. She now writes full time and lives with her partner of twenty-two years, two dogs and five cats, all of whom she rescued.

If you would like to be kept up to date with new releases from J. New, you can sign up to her *Reader's Group* on her website www.jnewwrites.com You will also receive a link to download the free e-book, *The Yellow Cottage Mystery*, the short-story prequel to The Yellow Cottage Vintage Mystery series.

Printed in Great Britain
by Amazon

66217268R00095